Death at the Lighthouse

By John Reisinger

Glyphworks Publishing

Death at the Lighthouse
A Max Hurlock Roaring 20s Mystery
www.johnreisinger.com

This book is a work of fiction. Except for specific historic references, names, characters, places and incidents are products of the author's imagination and are not to be construed as real, and any resemblance to any actual place, event, organization or person living or dead, is unintentional and purely coincidental.

All rights reserved. No part of this book may be reproduced in any form or by any means without the prior written consent of the author or publisher, except for brief quotes to be used in reviews.

Copyright 2012 by John Reisinger
ISBN 978-0-9838818-3-4
Glyphworks Publishing, LLC
2012

To my wife and research partner Barbara, who helps get the Hurlocks off the ground and into print.

Acknowledgements

I would like to thank the following for their help:

The Chesapeake Bay Maritime Museum, St Michaels, Maryland

The Mayor's Office, Crisfield, Maryland

The Crisfield Police Department

Tim Howard, The Tawes Museum, Crisfield, Maryland

The Somerset County Public Library

The Talbot County Library

Whitey Schmidt

Larry Antenick

H.P. Ketterman

Louise Dolan

Jennifer Bodine, www.aaubreybodine.com

Cast of Characters

St Michaels:
Max and Allison Hurlock
J.D. Pratt and Casper Nowitsky-watermen
Isis Dalrymple-librarian
Duffy Merkle-farmer, moonshiner
Thelma Lonnigan-telephone operator
Mabel Johnson-widow
Madame DeSousa-spiritualist

Crisfield:
Detective Sergeant Fred Bentley- Crisfield Police
Jack Coleman- lighthouse keeper
Tom and Nell Paisley- speakeasy owners
Billy Thebold- Nell Paisley's friend
Brian Murphy- rumrunner
Rufus Grace- waterman, part-time rumrunner
Gaston Means- federal agent

Baltimore:
Hal Marks- reporter
Irene Sterling- spiritualist
Dr. Osgood and Beatrice Winslow- Allison's parents
Lieutenant Scheffel-US Coast Guard
Master Chief Voshel-US Coast Guard
Mr. Collins- séance attendee

Author's note:

Maryland's Eastern Shore, that part of the state on the eastern side of the Chesapeake Bay, has long had its own culture, history and traditions. Until the construction of the Chesapeake Bay Bridge in 1952, the agricultural Eastern Shore might as well have been an island as far as the rest of the state was concerned. From Baltimore and Annapolis, it could only be reached by water, unless you were willing to take a long and indirect journey north and then south over a piecemeal road system.

The result was a place that resembled the rural south as much as anything. The biggest industries were farming the land and harvesting the bay. In the 1920s, canneries shipped oysters from the water and tomatoes from the land. Watermen harvested oysters in the cooler weather and hauled produce for sale to Baltimore and Annapolis in the summer.

Towns such as St Michaels and Oxford shifted from shipbuilding to seafood production by the end of the 1800s and Crisfield became the oyster capitol of the world.

Because of Prohibition, however, many watermen were tempted to use their boats and their skills for some very profitable rumrunning. This was made possible by the vast network of rivers and ragged coastline coupled with a smuggling and blockade running tradition that dated back to before the Civil War.

Death at the Lighthouse

Baltimore

MARYLAND

Annapolis

Washington

Claiborne • St Michaels

DELAWARE

Cambridge

Ocean City

Devil's Elbow light

Crisfield

VIRGINIA

The Chesapeake Bay
1924

Other books by John Reisinger

Master Detective

Master Detective (Updated and expanded edition)

Evasive Action

Nassau

The Duckworth Chronicles

The Max Hurlock Roaring 20s Mysteries:

Death of a Flapper

Death on a Golden Isle

Death at the Lighthouse

And coming in 2013:

Death and the Blind Tiger

The Confessions of Gonzalo Guererro

Titus McTeague and the Crown of Mexico

Chapter 1

Local Celebrities

Allison Hurlock gently squeezed a tomato at the St Michaels general store, then put it in a sack. The store clerk looked on approvingly.

"Those are prime tomatoes Miss Allison. They're grown right up the road near Unionville."

"They must have the knack," Allison replied. "Mine sort of withered on the vine while Max and I were off on investigations. I think they died of thirst."

The clerk wiped his hands on his apron. "You know I heard about some of those investigations. Max solved that case with that society couple shot to death in a locked room. Mercy! Just like in those dime novels. So what happened? It was the butler that did it, wasn't it?"

Allison smiled and picked out another tomato.

"Sorry, but there wasn't any butler to blame, not even a housemaid."

"And that poisoning case in that club for rich people in Georgia last winter..."

"The Jekyll Island Club."

"Right. They must have had butlers there."

"They had a few, but none of them killed anyone. Still, Max got to the bottom of the case even without them."

"Why, here he is now," said the grocer, hearing the screen door squeak and slam shut.

"Afternoon, Henry," said Max. "Got any Rockfish today?"

"I'm way ahead of you, Max," said Allison. "Henry has a nice one all wrapped and ready to go as soon as I get enough tomatoes. Ah, that's enough. Now let's pay the nice man and head on back."

Henry the clerk took the money and gave Allison the change.

"You'll like those tomatoes, folks. They're set aside special. The rest of them go straight to the cannery. Say, are you investigating any more murders now?"

Max shook his head. "Not a chance. We're still getting caught up from all the time we spent out of town on the ones we've already had fall in our laps. I think we'll stick with our air service for a while and leave chasing criminals to the police."

The clerk tried to hide his disappointment as the screen door slammed once again.

The main street of St Michaels was hot under a late fall sun. The leaves had started to turn and the corn was almost ready to harvest. Local children were working on Halloween costumes, and down at the boatyard, people were hauling out boats for the coming winter.

"It appears we've become minor celebrities around here, Max. All everyone wants to talk about is solving murders."

"Pure sensationalism," Max grumbled. "Nothing makes for better gossip than sex and violence. It'll die down soon enough without anything new to feed it. Meanwhile, I guess we'll just have to ignore it."

"Typical modesty," Allison replied. "You're just doing the old 'aw, shucks' act to show how humble you are. It's all right. You can admit it; you enjoy the attention."

"I do not."

"Says you. Why, Duffy Merkle was practically asking for your autograph last week to show his moonshiner friends, and I saw you grinning when Isis Dalrymple went all goo goo eyed at you about it yesterday at the library. I half-expected her to sigh and say 'my hero'. That sure looked enjoyable to me."

"All right, all right. I suppose basking in admiration isn't entirely unpleasant, but I'm just afraid that everyone will think I'm some sort of private eye now. Next thing you know they'll want me to spy on someone's husband or help them find a lost cat."

"That reminds me," said Allison, snapping her fingers. "I've got a deadline coming up on that article I'm writing on spiritualism."

"How does my newfound status as small-town celebrity semi-detective remind you of spiritualism?"

"Well, last week I interviewed a woman who was using a Ouija board to find her lost cat."

"I had to ask."

"She had a few friends over and they all placed their hands on the planchette, that's the sliding thing that points out the letters. After a while they had a message."

"They actually got a message from a cat? What did it say?"

"It said something like grthh, sjik, bsds. The ladies were very disappointed."

"Cats are notoriously bad at spelling, I suppose. So they never found the feline?" said Max.

"Actually, they did. It was asleep on the back porch."

"Another triumph for spiritualism. Well, at least they didn't ask me to whip out a magnifying glass and find it by deduction."

They had reached the Model T and placed the groceries in the back. Max got in and started the engine, which responded with a roar and a shudder. They passed through the rest of the town, past the Episcopal Church, past the post office, and past the canneries at Navy Point. They continued their discussion as they drove, their voices vibrating slightly with the bouncing of the suspension over the oyster-shell road.

"Up until a few weeks ago I was Max Hurlock, local Eastern Shore boy, airplane jockey, and engineer. The only thing I was famous for was going off to college; well, that and marrying a Western Shore Goucher girl who looks like that movie star Mary Miles Minter."

"Why, Max; you'll make me blush."

"I doubt it. Anyway, I don't want everyone with an overactive imagination beating a path to our door with murder rumors every time someone hasn't seen his neighbor around for a few days."

Allison laughed. "Oh, I don't know. A couple of creative wild goose chases might produce some good material for my next magazine article."

"Well, that makes me feel better."

"All this private eye talk adds some excitement at least," said Allison. "I remember when we got married you told me that almost everyone on Maryland's Eastern Shore raised either tomatoes or chickens from the land, or oysters from the bay. And the ones that don't usually work in canneries and packing houses processing the products of the ones that do."

"And the point is...?"

"The point is that, strange as it may seem, around here we're considered exotic."

They turned down the lane that led to their house.

"Look, Max," Allison said, in her 'reasonable' tone, "Maybe you're right; maybe soon it'll become yesterday's news and things will get back to normal. I mean, it's not like people are waiting at our door with new cases to solve."

"That would be very reassuring," said Max, "except for one thing."

"Oh? And what's that?"

Max pointed at their house, appearing through the trees. Two men were sitting on the front porch waiting for them to return.

John Reisinger

Chapter 2

Acting strange

"Max, what do they want and who are they?"

"I have no idea what they want, but I know who they are; Casper Nowitsky and J.D. Pratt. I've known them since I was a kid. They're watermen. One of them probably caught that Rockfish we bought. I haven't seen them since before you and I got married."

The Model T pulled up at the porch steps and the visitors stood up. Max greeted them with a nod.

"Hey Casper. Hey, J.D."

"Hey, Max," they replied in unison.

"Oh, Allison, may I present Mr. Casper Nowitsky, otherwise known as No Whiskey, and Mr. J.D. Pratt, otherwise known as Five by Five. Gentlemen, this is my bride, Allison."

The watermen seemed momentarily stunned, and stood slightly open-mouthed for a second or two. Allison often had that effect on men.

"I'm real sorry we missed the wedding, Miss Allison," said Casper, who was the first to recover, "but it was duck season and…"

"…and we were up at the flats with a sneak boat. Wish we'd had a market gun. The canvasbacks were as thick as…"

"Why do they call you five by five, Mr. Pratt?" said Allison, in an attempt to break the awkwardness.

Pratt blushed slightly. "Well, see, I'm a little big-boned."

"Don't let that fool you Miss Allison," said Casper. "Ol' J.D.'s built like a beer barrel, but he's strong as an ox. He can haul up a skipjack sail all by hisself."

"And you, Mr. Nowitsky. Why do they call you no whiskey?"

"Well in my younger days, back before Prohibition, I used to get a little tight on Saturday nights. After a while, when the local bars saw me coming they'd say 'No whiskey for Nowitsky.'"

"Never mind that, Allison," Max interrupted. "As fascinating as their sordid histories might be, I'm sure Casper and J.D. Have other things on their mind."

"That's right, Max. We surely do."

"Come on in and have a seat. We'll get the groceries put away in the ice box then we'll talk."

A few minutes later they were all seated in the parlor. The late afternoon air was cooler and the electric fan hummed in the corner making the room comfortable. Casper Nowitsky spoke first.

"Max, the thing is this; we heard about how you solved those murder cases and we always knew you were a smart fella, so we weren't surprised."

Max sighed. "And you have a case for me to solve. Right?"

J.D. Pratt took over. "Not a case, Max, just a...Well, let's just say we got us a concern."

"A concern? Say, I've known you boys since grammar school. You never have a concern about anything except drudging, tonging and gunning. What gives?"

"Well," Casper began, "J.D. and me were out in the Karen Rebecca tonging for arsters down in Tangier Sound towards Crisfield."

"Arsters?" said Allison.

"Oysters," said Max, translating from the original Eastern Shore. "Go ahead. What happened?"

"Well, you know that storm that came up this afternoon? Well, the wind was blowing out of the nor'east somethin' fierce, so we figured we'd hole up until it blowed over."

Max nodded, but said nothing.

"Well, we were just a mile or so from the Devil's Elbow light down near Crisfield, so we figured we'd drop in on Jack Coleman, the light keeper. We figured that ol' boy could use some company and we could use a place to hole up for an hour or so before heading the rest of the way back to Tilghman."

"Very sensible," said Max.

"Well, Devil's Elbow is a screw-pile light. You know, a six-sided house with a steel frame underneath. So we tie up below and make the Karen Rebecca secure and climb the ladder to the platform that goes around the house. First thing we notice is the door's locked. Now we think what would a man in a lighthouse miles from shore need with a locked door?"

"We thought it was a mite peculiar," Casper added, somewhat unnecessarily.

"Anyway, we knock on the door and hear a voice say 'who's there?' real threatening-like. By this time the rain and the wind was kickin' up pretty good and we were getting soaked out there. Finally, Jack Coleman opened the door and he was standing there with a knife in his hand, like he thought we were pirates or something. He finally let us in and settled down, but Max, he was all in a sweat about something."

"Or someone," said Casper Nowitsky. "When we asked him what spooked him, he just laughed it off. Said he wasn't used to visitors."

"And you think it was something else? Something sinister?" said Max.

J.D. shrugged. "Max, we don't know what to think. All we know is that the Jack Coleman we'd see in town occasionally wasn't the man we saw at the lighthouse. We ain't saying he's an imposter or anything. That was him sure enough; he just acted different. We think he's either in trouble of some sort, or hiding something."

"Interesting," Max said non-committedly, "but what do you want me to do? Why not talk to the Crisfield police about it?"

"We did," said J.D. "We stopped in to Crisfield and told the police what happened. They just said that being nervous wasn't against the law. Told us to forget it."

"Sounds like good advice to me," said Max.

"That's because you didn't see him, Max. I'm telling you, that man was scared."

"Which brings me back to my original question," said Max. "What do you expect me to do about it?"

"Look Max, you know more about detective work than we do, and you can find out what's really going on most of the time. How about coming out there with us tomorrow and see him for yourself? Maybe you can get him to talk about it, or maybe see some clues to figure out what's wrong."

"But..." Max began to protest.

"The Karen Rebecca's tied up at the ferry dock in Claiborne just a few miles down the road. From there, we could get you out to the Devil's Elbow in maybe three hours. We can leave first thing tomorrow."

Max looked over at Allison, who smiled. "It's lovely weather for a nice boat ride down the bay, Max. I'll pack you a lunch."

J.D. and Casper grinned.

"All right," Max sighed, "but I'm not guaranteeing anything. Remember; detective work is one thing, but mind reading is something else entirely."

After Casper and J.D. had gone, Max and Allison sat on their porch sipping lemonade and listening to the crickets and the ducks squawking in the distance as the sun went down.

"So Max," Allison said, turning toward him, "What was that bushwa about market guns and sneak boats? More of the mysteries of the Eastern Shore?"

Max nodded. "Sort of. The flats he was talking about are the Susquehanna flats up at the northern tip of the Chesapeake Bay where the Susquehanna River dumps in. There's a huge shallow area there that is full of canvasback ducks this time of year. A sneak boat is a small boat that floats almost flush with the water, so the ducks can't see it until it's too late."

"And a market gun?"

"The biggest shotgun you ever saw; almost a cannon. It takes two men to handle it and it kicks like a mule, but it can take down dozens of ducks at one time."

"Sounds awful."

"It is for the ducks, but the gunners can bag a big catch pretty quickly."

"Still, I'm surprised they allow it."

"They don't. Market guns have been illegal since 1910. The problem is, it's so profitable some of the old gunners still use them when they can get away with it."

"Sounds like Prohibition. Well, I hope you have a good time tomorrow with your very interesting friends," said Allison. She frowned, suddenly remembering something else. "Wait a minute; that explains what gunning is, but what did you mean by ...what was it...drudging and tonging?"

"Drudging is local talk for dredging; dragging a sort of cage over the bottom to scoop up oysters. Tonging is the old way; picking them up off the bottom with tongs. Tongs are sort of scissor-like contraptions with claws on the ends."

"Sounds like a tough way to earn a living," said Allison.

"It's brutal and dangerous; especially in the winter. Before I went in the navy, I helped Casper and J.D. a few times when they were shorthanded. I'd never want to do it again, but most of these watermen wouldn't want to do anything else."

"Very commendable," said Allison. "Nothing like freezing and risking your life so palookas in bars can slurp some slimy sea creatures. You should have a grand time with those boys when they take you out tomorrow."

"Tomorrow. I knew it; this is exactly what I was afraid was going to happen," Max grumbled, staring straight ahead into the deepening shadows and gesturing with his glass. "Casper and J.D. get spooked because a lighthouse keeper didn't welcome them the way they thought they deserved, so they go running off to me. If I wasn't suddenly the great local gumshoe, they would have just forgotten about it. So what am I supposed to do; get out my magnifying glass and examine Coleman's cigar ash? Then I gather all the suspects in the library and pronounce the solution?" Max's voice rose in exasperation. "For the love of Pete, there isn't even a crime!"

"Oh, I don't know," Allison chuckled. "Is overacting a crime?"

"I'm serious," Max insisted. "I'm being asked to investigate someone's state of mind."

"Well," said Allison, "you have to admit the light keeper acted pretty crackers when Casper and J.D. showed up."

"Look. You've met Casper and J.D. If they showed up unannounced at your front door in a storm, how would you act?"

"Good point. Those two would make a grizzly bear nervous."

Max sighed. "Well, I guess running out to the light is harmless enough. The weather is supposed to be good and it'll be a nice trip. Jack Coleman will probably act normally and the boys will think I'm a genius."

"And then they'll tell everyone and you'll have even more clients."

Max put down his glass. "Oh no. I hadn't thought of that."

Allison rose and walked over to Max's chair. She sat on his lap and wrapped her arms around his neck and kissed him.

"The price of fame, darling; but you bear it so bravely. How you must suffer."

Max pulled her closer. "I really do. But you know, suddenly I'm feeling a whole lot better."

She kissed him again, then whispered in his ear.

"To paraphrase Al Jolson, you ain't seen nothin' yet."

John Reisinger

Chapter 3

The Devil's Elbow

The next morning, Allison remained at home behind the typewriter working on her article on spiritualism while Max prepared reluctantly for his trip to the lighthouse.

"I'm sure you and the good old boys will have a much better time without me tagging along," she told him. "No need to overwhelm the keeper with a crowd of uninvited guests. If two people spook him, four might make him jump in the bay."

Max nodded. "I should be back by late this afternoon. I figure three hours to get to the light, an hour visit, then three hours back. Maybe around four or so. Will you be home?"

"I'm not sure yet," said Allison, rustling through some notes. "I may go into town or up to Easton for another interview for my spiritualism article if I can get some information on Madame DeSousa from Isis Dalrymple. That way I can ask her some good questions."

"It seems we're both chasing shadows. Well, if I need you maybe I can call you by telepathy."

The Karen Rebecca was tied up at the steamship wharf in nearby Claiborne. She was an old solid deadrise workboat, the kind that resembled oversized rowboats with small cabins near the bow and plenty of deck space for working on the water. The boat smelled of fish, oysters and gasoline, and was badly in need of a fresh coat of paint. One area along the rail was worn down to the bare gray wood from Casper and J.D. hauling oyster tongs and crab traps over it. Twin exhaust pipes jutted upwards at a rakish angle from the amidships engine.

"Hey, this is like old times, Max; like when we went out on the water together."

"Yeah," said Max under his breath, " and I didn't like it then either."

J.D. started the engine with a rumble and a cloud of oily black smoke, and nodded approvingly. "She's runnin' smooth today."

"Obviously," said Max, suppressing a cough. "I just hope I live to be as old as this boat."

"All right, Max. I'll just take off the bow line and we'll be on our way."

The boat headed out of the harbor into Eastern Bay and turned south past Poplar Island, a low area slowly sinking and eroding from the elements. Soon they were passing the mouth of the Choptank River and spotted the white sails of Skipjack workboats.

"They're drudging over towards that bar," said J.D., squinting in the sunlight, "but that spot's pretty played out about now. You got to go south to get the good beds. That's why we were there yesterday."

Max nodded. "How did you do?"

"Thirty bushels. Of course the storm cut us short."

"Does it get crowded down there?"

"Not too bad. There's plenty of boats from Crisfield, but the place is big enough for everybody. 'Course we got to watch out for drudgers sneakin' up from Virginia."

"What do you do then?"

J.D. motioned to the small pilot house on the boat. There, in a rack below the window, was the dark form of a double barreled shotgun.

"We try to discourage 'em."

Max looked at the shotgun for a moment.

"Have you used it?"

"You mean on a Virginia drudger?"

"On anyone."

"Well, I ain't actually pulled the trigger on 'em, but I waved it around a few times. It gets their attention."

"I'll bet."

Mile after mile of rippled water passed under the hull as the long low lying green shoreline drifted steadily past. They saw a steamboat on the horizon heading north, probably the Norfolk-Baltimore run. Black smoke drifted from its stack and made a smudge on the horizon. Later they saw several Skipjacks, the graceful sail powered workboats, clustered around a buy boat to sell their catch directly to a middleman.

Finally, they turned around a finger of land and saw the Devil's Elbow light, a speck in the distance. As they got closer, they saw another boat that seemed to be heading for the light as well.

"What do you make of that, Max?"

Max peered through an ancient pair of binoculars.

"Looks like the police," said Max. "What do you think, J.D.?"

"I do believe that's Detective Sergeant Fred Bentley from the Crisfield Police," said J.D. "That's who we talked to yesterday. What's he doing way out here? Casper, can you intercept him?"

"No sweat," said Casper, swinging the wheel slightly. A few minutes later, they were able to hail the boat and pull up alongside."

"Well, if it ain't Five by Five and No Whiskey. Morning, boys," said Sergeant Bentley, a thin, dark-haired man in his early forties. "Say, is that Max Hurlock? You look like married life agrees with you, Max."

"That's me, Fred. Where are you headed?"

Bentley pushed his hat back slightly on his head. "Oh, I'm just taking me a little run to the Devil's Elbow light."

"That's where we're headed. We can go together. Give Jack Coleman a real party."

"So is something going on at the light, Fred?" Max asked.

"Probably not, but we got a couple of calls early this morning that the light wasn't on last night. Of course that's really the job of the Lighthouse Service, but things were a little slow today, so the mayor thought it wouldn't hurt to have a look."

Max smiled. "Elections coming up next month, eh?"

Sergeant Bentley smiled slyly. "Now, Max; I'm sure he's just keeping the taxpayers happy is all. Anyway, here I am."

Casper and J.D. anxiously reminded Bentley of their experience the day before.

"Yeah, I remember you boys told me about your visit. One of our Crisfield watermen told me he saw your boat tied up at the light long about one or two yesterday, so I guess that was you."

"That was us, all right," said J.D., "just like we said. But why would the light be out?"

"I try not to have an opinion unless I have some facts," said Bentley. "Who do you think I am, the mayor?"

"Well..."

"All I know," he continued, "is that that's an important light. If it isn't on, people notice."

"Have you had any reports of the light being out before?" Max asked.

Sergeant Bentley shook his head. "Not a one. Jack Coleman is pretty reliable. Still, he could have had a problem with the lens or maybe the kerosene supply. It happens. Nothing to do but go out there and see. Then I can set the mayor's mind at ease."

"Wouldn't it be easier to just call him on the radio and ask him about the light?" Max asked.

Bentley shook his head. "I already tried that. He isn't answering."

Allison looked through her notes for her spiritualism article and found she still hadn't been able to talk to Easton's top medium, Madame DeSousa. She had one of Madame DeSousa's handbills and noticed she gave séances on weekends and "spiritual instruction" on weekdays. She placed a call to the phone number on the handbill and was pleased to hear the call answered by Madame DeSousa herself.

"Why, yes, Mrs. Hurlock. You say you are writing for a magazine? I'd be glad to talk to you about spiritual things, as long as you use my name in your article."

Allison assured her she would use the name if she used any quotes or material, and Madame DeSousa agreed to meet later that day.

Allison cranked the telephone and asked Thelma the operator to put her through to Isis Dalrymple at the library in town. In addition to being the town's part-time librarian and wife of the biggest tomato farmer in the area, Isis was the local know-it-all, who acted as sort of a human encyclopedia for St Michaels. Although she often volunteered knowledge without being asked to, and in far more detail than was needed, she was generally considered a good egg.

"Hey, Isis. This is Allison Hurlock."

"Hail, Allison. Are you perchance thirsting after enlightenment this fine day?"

Isis Dalrymple talked like that. People said it was the result of her extensive reading coupled with being named for an Egyptian goddess.

"Aren't we all?" said Allison. "In fact, that's what I'm calling about. I'm interviewing a spiritualist up in Easton, a certain Madame DeSousa. Any chance you could find some background information on her in the reference section?"

"The St Michaels library is better known for what it doesn't have than what it does, I fear," said Isis. "All we carry are some old clipping files from the Star-Democrat. I seem to remember reading something about Madame DeSousa somewhere, though. Let me cogitate upon the matter and see what I can glean from the old cerebral cortex."

"Thanks, Isis. When it comes to research, you're the eel's eyebrows. No need to make a big project out of it, but if you find anything, could you give me a call? I'll be here until noon. Thanks a lot."

"Sure, Allison. As Plato said, 'Knowledge is the food of the soul'."

"I'll tell my editor that."

Allison looked over her notes with satisfaction. If Isis could dig up something juicy on Madame DeSousa, this could be an interesting interview.

The Devil's Elbow light appeared first as a smudge in the haze; then solidified into a red-roofed one story hexagonal building supported about ten feet above the water by a frame of steel columns and braces. Waves lazily lapped against the supports and a lone seagull slowly rode a wind current overhead.
"I don't see anybody yet," said J.D.
"Maybe he's inside trying to fix the light," said Max. "We'll know soon enough."
J.D. raised a pair of binoculars to his eyes.
"Well don't that beat all?"
"What is it?" said Max.
J.D. handed the binoculars to Max.
"He left the door open. Shoot. Yesterday he had the thing locked and today it's wide open. He's liable to get a seagull flying in there and stealing his lunch if he isn't careful."
Max examined the lighthouse, now appearing larger as the boat got closer.
"Maybe there was a fire that damaged the light and Coleman's airing the place out."
"Can you see inside?" Casper asked.
Max shook his head. "No. The angle is wrong and so is the light. We'll just have to get closer."
As the two boats came up to the light, Sergeant Bentley in the next boat stood up and cupped his hands over his mouth.
"Ahoy there at the light. This is Detective Sergeant Fred Bentley of the Crisfield Police speaking. Is everything all right in there?"

There was no answer, only the lapping of the waves and the monotonous throb of the motor.

The Karen Rebecca bumped gently against a piling and stopped alongside a small platform close to the water level. Sergeant Bentley's smaller boat did the same. Casper and J.D. cut the engine and tied up the boat as Max and the Sergeant Bentley stepped off and started to climb the ladder to the platform that surrounded the building.

There was still no sound from inside the station.

"I don't mind telling you, Max; this is getting spooky," said Bentley.

"Either Coleman is hard of hearing, or he isn't here," said Max. "That is, unless..."

"Unless what?"

"Never mind. Now my imagination is getting carried away."

They reached the platform. Casper and J.D. were close behind by this time, but no one spoke. They all stopped for a moment, listening, but heard nothing.

"Mr. Coleman? Jack?" Bentley shouted as they made their way along the deck toward the open door.

Max and Bentley stepped into the doorway at the same time and looked around.

"What the hell?" said Bentley.

Casper and J.D. had caught up, and crowded in behind them.

"Damn," said Casper almost reverently.

"Holy..." said J.D.

The room was pie shaped, with two walls radiating outward from the lighthouse's center staircase. The floor was dark pine planks, but the walls and ceiling were painted white. The place looked as if it had been the scene of a riot. A desk in the corner was pushed out of place and the chair was turned over. Papers from the desk were scattered around the room and rustled softly in the breeze from the open doorway. The radio set was overturned and broken on the floor.

There was no sign of the lighthouse keeper.

"Well, that might explain why he wasn't answering your call on the radio, Fred," said Max.

"Yeah, but where is he?"

Max felt a numbness in the pit of his stomach, but fought the feeling.

"We'd better spread out and see if Coleman is here somewhere and what condition he's in," said Max, moving toward the next room on the left. Sergeant Bentley headed toward the room on the right.

The next room Max came to was almost identical; furniture overturned and some papers scattered on the floor, but no lighthouse keeper. In the room was a stove, which Max noted was cold. A nearby table was set for one, but with two white porcelain coffee mugs. Max saw that the plate was clean, but there was some coffee in each of the mugs. He heard Bentley call from the room on the other side.

"Oh, my God! He's in here, Max."

Max rushed back and into the room on the other side to find Sergeant Bentley, Casper and J. D. standing open mouthed and slightly green. On the floor was the crumpled body of Jack Coleman, lighthouse keeper of the Devil's Elbow light.

John Reisinger

Chapter 4

The body in question

    Sergeant Bentley was bent over the lighthouse keeper feeling for a pulse when Max arrived.
    "He's dead," said Bentley. "The body's cold, so he's been dead for hours. There's a knife over here under that chair, and look; there's a puddle of blood right by the body. Someone must have broken in here and stabbed him."
    Max was looking at the body now. He rolled the keeper over and inspected carefully.
    "I'd better get back and send the coroner out here," said Bentley, "and maybe the funeral home people as well. But first I'll get someone to take some pictures."
    "There's a partial footprint here," said Max. "Looks like somebody stepped in the puddle by the body. Better make sure that gets photographed."
    Casper and J.D. were both shaking their heads.
    "I told you this old boy was afraid of somethin'. Looks like he had reason to be."

Max had left the body and was looking at the front door. He started looking through the papers fluttering on the floor.

"So, Max," said J.D. "Do you agree with Sergeant Bentley?"

Max looked up absent-mindedly. "Agree? Oh, yes. We have to get the coroner and the funeral home people out here as soon as possible. I'd also suggest notifying the Lighthouse Service so they can make arrangements to get Devil's Elbow light back in service."

"I don't mean that," J.D. insisted. "I mean do you agree that someone broke in here and stabbed ol' Jack Coleman?"

"Well, it's early yet. We don't really know for sure..."

Sergeant Bentley looked at Max. "Come on Max. J.D.'s right. I want to know what you really think. If this case is going to get solved, we need all the brain power we can get. You solved those cases out of state, so maybe you can help out here. I won't be offended. I'm a big boy."

Max took a deep breath. "Well, here's what I see. Coleman wasn't stabbed to death. There's a nasty spot on the side of his head that indicates he was killed by a hard blow to the head."

"But what about the blood?" said Bentley.

"The blood you see belonged to the killer. What's more, the killer didn't break in; Coleman let him in. Coleman knew the killer, although he wasn't expecting him. Whatever happened didn't happen right away. They had some sort of falling out that resulted in a scuffle or fight where Coleman was killed and the killer wounded. Oh, and the killer was looking for something in Coleman's papers."

The room was silent for a moment. Outside, a gull screeched somewhere overhead.

Sergeant Bentley let out a breath of air. "Well, at least I got the name of the victim right. Are you sure about this Max?"

Max shrugged his shoulders. "I'm afraid so."

"Damn," said Casper. "But how do you know, Max?"

"Yes," said Sergeant Bentley. "I'd like to know myself."

"Look. I'm not trying to upstage you, Fred, but I have to draw inferences from what I see..."

"Just get on with it, Max," said Sergeant Bentley, waving his hand. "How do you know?"

"Well, it was cool on the bay yesterday, so the windows are all closed and locked. The front door has two locks, but neither one has been thrown, and there is no sign of scratches or broken wood on the door jamb, so it looks like whoever dropped by was admitted freely and did not break in. I examined the body and there was no stab wound I could find, and no blood on the floor under the body. Plus there are some small blood spots on the front of Coleman's shirt, and a few small spots here and there on the floor, so the blood must be from the killer, probably from a wound inflicted by Coleman with the knife you found."

"There has to be a knife wound, Max," Bentley insisted. "Maybe you just missed it. The coroner will be able to find it."

Max shook his head, "No, he won't. Sorry."

"I suppose the front door told you that Coleman knew the killer, too?" asked Bentley.

"Partly," said Max, "but there's more. In the next room is a table with two half-filled coffee mugs, indicating that Coleman knew whoever was here and sat talking with him for a while. There is also a plate with a knife, fork, and napkin next to it; dinner set for one. That tells me that whoever dropped in did so without notice, since Coleman was getting ready to make his dinner, but was interrupted and had coffee with his visitor instead."

"All right," said Bentley, "and I suppose the papers scattered around indicate the killer was looking for something in them?"

Max nodded. "In fact, the killer even went through Coleman's pockets, apparently. It looks like Coleman wounded the killer slightly and the killer was dripping blood slowly. I think the puddle formed when the bleeding killer knelt by the body to go through the pockets. Then when he stood up again, he stepped in the puddle and left the footprint."

"Wait," said Casper. "Maybe the papers just got thrown out when the desk was knocked sideways in the struggle. It don't mean anyone was looking through them."

"Look a little closer," said Max, pointing to the desk. "The desk was pushed sideways a few feet, but every drawer has been pulled open. No, someone had to have done that intentionally to look for something."

"Do you suppose he found it?"

Max didn't answer right away. He was looking at the desk and its papers. Finally, he turned to Sergeant Bentley.

"Yes, I think he did find what he was looking for."

"But how in the world..."

"Never mind that now, Fred," said Max calmly. "I think we need to get the coroner out here, along with some people from your office to secure the scene. And we need to let the Lighthouse Service know."

Sergeant Bentley looked a little dazed, but recovered quickly. "Yes, Max; you're right. I need to get back right away."

"And," Max added, "We need to post someone here until you get some police out here in case Mr. Coleman has any more visitors. Casper and J.D. and I can stay here until you get back."

J.D. nodded. "Sure thing, Max."

"All right," said Bentley. "Let's see how fast I can get back to Crisfield. But first, Max, I want to know just what it was that the killer was looking for and why you think he found it."

"I know he found it because it isn't here," said Max.

"What isn't here?"

"The keeper's logbook."

Sergeant Bentley slowly nodded. "And the logbook has a record of everyone who visits or is in contact with the light."

"Not to mention any ships that pass by or anything unusual the keeper sees," added Max.

"Like rumrunners, maybe?" said Sergeant Bentley. "That sounds like a pretty good motive for murder to me."

"As you said, Fred, it's no good having an opinion until you have the facts."

Sergeant Bentley got back in his boat and took off for Crisfield. As the sound of Bentley's boat faded, J.D. turned nervously to Max.

"Well, don't this just beat all? Stuck in a danged lighthouse with a dead man. What are we going to do now?"

"I don't know about you," Max replied, "but I'm going to have another look around."

Chapter 5

Allison visits the Spirit World

After Isis Dalrymple called her back with some background information on Madame DeSousa, Allison took the Model T and headed up the road towards Easton. Max hadn't returned, of course and she didn't expect him back until much later.

"He and the good ol' boys are probably comparing fishing stories and forgot the time," she chuckled to herself. "Well, we'll both have stories to tell tonight."

The flivver chugged through St Michaels and over the bridge at Newcomb. A little later, Allison was in Easton.

Easton was a fairly big place compared to St Michaels, but then again, most places were. By any other measure Easton was a small colonial town, with most activity centering around the old Talbot County Courthouse on South Washington Street. In front of the courthouse was a statue dedicated to Talbot County men who had served in the Confederacy during the Civil War. Max had told her that people in favor of a similar statue honoring those who served the Union had not been able to raise the money for a statue, so the Confederate monument stood alone. Allison noticed that the figure on the statue carried a furled flag, but no weapons of any kind, and wondered if it was the sculptor's way of downplaying the war's violence and tragedy.

Madame DeSousa's house was a trim Victorian affair on Goldsborough Street, marked only by a brass plaque on the front door that said simply, "Madame DeSousa, Spiritualist".

Allison rang the bell and a moment later, the door opened and a gray-haired woman who appeared to be in her 60s answered. She was not as tall as Allison and a little more compact in build. She wore an old-fashioned dress with a floor length skirt. The woman didn't speak at first but just stood looking intently at Allison for a few seconds.

"You are Allison Hurlock," said the woman. "I am Madame DeSousa. I sense you are a skeptic regarding the spirit world."

"Well, I…"

"Oh, that's all right. Many people start out that way, but ultimately come to the truth. I don't mind. Come in and sit down."

She led Allison into a tastefully-appointed parlor with red velvet curtains and dark brown overstuffed furniture. Allison sat in a soft chair and noticed a Ouija board on a small table nearby next to a stuffed owl.

"You may proceed Allison. Ask me any question you like. If I don't have the answer, the spirits will provide it." Madame DeSousa half sat, half reclined on an overstuffed blue velvet loveseat, like some Middle Eastern potentate.

"Thank you for talking to me, Madame DeSousa," Allison began. "What can you tell me about being a medium?"

"Well, Allison," Madame DeSousa spoke with slow sweeping hand gestures, "the spirit world is all around us, and the spirits of the departed are just beyond the reach of most people, but a few of us are fortunate enough to be mediums. That means we provide a channel between the spirits of the departed and those left behind."

Allison nodded. "I see. And do you hear them now, or do you need a séance?"

"The purpose of a séance is to focus the contact to specific spirits, relatives of the attendees and so forth, but I hear the spirits all the time."

"Now?"

"Oh, yes. The air is filled with their soft voices. As Caliban said in The Tempest, 'The isle is full of noises, sounds and sweet airs that give delight and hurt not.' The spirits tell me everything about the universe. They have all knowledge, you see, and are anxious to communicate that knowledge to a medium."

"That must be very handy," said Allison, "like your own invisible encyclopedia."

"Why, what a charming way of putting it. That's how I knew you were Allison before you even told me, and how I knew you were a skeptic. The spirits also tell me you are a Goucher graduate, your maiden name is Winslow, and your husband has had great success in solving crimes."

"The spirits are pretty thorough," Alison remarked.

Madame De Sousa smiled. "For the spirits, such knowledge is almost trivial."

"There is one thing I'm really curious about, though," said Allison.

Madame DeSousa nodded graciously. "Of course."

"Why do you have a doorbell?"

"I beg your pardon?" Madame De Sousa looked confused.

"Well, if you're constantly surrounded by all-knowing spirits just itching to tell you everything, couldn't one of them at least tell you when someone's at the door?"

"I...well,...the spirits are not servants, you know. I mean...well, look...I think we should stick to serious questions."

"Of course" said Allison, cheerfully. "What about séances? People come to you to talk to their dead relatives. So how do you know how to select the exact relative they want out of all those spirits floating around out there? I mean, I don't suppose they have labels."

Madame DeSousa was on more familiar ground now. "Well, my dear, as I explained, the spirits surround us, invisible in the air like the transmissions of those new Marconi devices one reads about."

"Radios, you mean?"

"Exactly. The medium acts as the Marconi receiver to filter out the unwanted part of the transmission and announce the results. I'm afraid I'm not sure how it works, but there it is."

"But don't the spirits sometimes appear as well?"

"They do. My séances frequently are visited by physical manifestations; trumpets, tambourines, disembodied hands, and even a ghost or two."

"And you can see them?"

"Oh, yes. And converse with them. They're telling me things about you even as we speak."

"About me? What are they telling you?"

Madame DeSousa swayed slightly and appeared to be looking off in space.

"There is a man in your life. I see a tall man..."

"You mean my husband Max?"

"Yes, Max. I see some sort of animal...a dog, perhaps?"

Allison shook her head. "No, we don't have a dog."

"Maybe a small child?"

"No."

"A brother or sister, perhaps.."

"I do have a brother."

"Well, there you are."

"But..."

"I see an older woman, a grandmother perhaps?"

"You tell me."

"This older woman passed away recently."

"Well, in 1917," said Allison.

"After a long illness?"

"About a week actually."

"That's right. A short illness, but a long time coming."

"A long time coming?"

"She wants you to know she's happy and wants you to be also."

"That's good to know. Say, can you ask her what she did with her apple pie recipe? My mother's been looking for it."

"She says you are a careful person, but can sometimes be impulsive," Madame DeSousa continued.

"Well..."

"You have some sort of a big decision coming up? Something to do with your husband's detective work?"

"Max doesn't have a case at the moment, so I don't see how..."

Madame DeSousa appeared to suddenly snap out of her semi trance. She looked surprised, as if she had just recalled something upsetting. She stared at Allison with eyes that did not seem quite focused. Allison nodded encouragement, but Madame DeSousa seemed to be looking right through her.

"Your husband will have another case sooner than you think, a case with danger where nothing is as it seems, and..."

In spite of herself, Allison felt a chill. "Yes?"

"...and you will be involved in it."

Chapter 6

Salt water

The lighthouse was strangely silent. Even the lapping of the waves against the supports seemed muffled. Max's footsteps on the wood plank floors seemed like gunshots in the quiet stillness.

He went into the room where the knife was found and looked at the weapon more closely. It was about ten inches long with a slight curvature. The handle was a hard wood, and the steel of the blade had a curious pattern of faint parallel wavy lines that seemed to be embedded in the metal. Max turned the knife over and examined it for any identifying marks, but there were none. Max stood up and walked to the stairway.

The rooms were arranged fan-like, around the enclosed center spiral stairway that led to the light.

"Max, you ain't going up there are you?" said J.D., who was hunched in a chair nervously looking out the window as if fearing another dead body would arrive any second.

"Thought I'd admire the view, J.D."

"You gonna just leave us with the body?"

"Now, J.D.; you don't expect me to take it with me, do you?"

"Hey, Max," came the voice of Casper. "I just come from the bathroom and somebody done stole the towels! What would a killer need with towels?"

"I imagine he used them to bandage his knife wound," said Max. "That would explain why we didn't find any spots of blood on the walkway or the outside stairs."

Max stepped into the stair enclosure as J.D was still protesting and Casper was looking for towels. The air was cooler here, a result of the chimney effect as warm air rose and drew cooler air in behind it. The steps creaked slightly as Max began to climb. The sun was higher now, and sunlight flooded into the glass enclosure at the top of the light, reflecting and distorting as it struck the huge glass lens that normally sent out beams at night. Max shaded his eyes against the glare.

To the west, the blue green waters of the Chesapeake stretched out to the opposite shore, with white work boats scattered across the waters and a gray plume of smoke from the stack of another white bay steamer drifting on the horizon. To the east were miles of marshes and wetland, a brown and green carpet interrupted here and there by patches of open water. Down below, the channel from the bay swept past the Devil's Elbow in a lazy curve that led to Crisfield in the hazy distance and over the horizon.

"A man could see a lot from up here," Max muttered to himself. "I wonder if Coleman might have seen too much?"

Max opened the access panel and stepped out on to the narrow walkway that formed a wooden collar around the top of the light. The wind was stronger and chilly. He looked down, then turned to go back inside. He was halfway through the access hatch when something caught his eye. Everything on and around the walkway had been painted multiple times, but there was a new and shiny wire running up to an equally new radio antenna.

"Hey Max," came the voice of J.D. from down below, "you all right up there?"

Max didn't want to tamper with any possible evidence, so he didn't touch the wire, but bent down and looked at it carefully.

"Max?"

J.D. had followed Max up the stairs and now appeared behind him. His eyes widened as he saw the wire.

"What you got there, Max?"

"It looks like a brand new radio wire and antenna."

"Well, shoot. I can see that, but what's it mean?"

"Probably nothing, but it's sort of a strange coincidence."

"A coincidence?"

Max nodded, still examining the antenna wire. "When a man is murdered and it comes the same time as some other unusual event, I have to wonder if there's a connection."

J.D. scratched his head. "What kind of a connection?"

"I don't know yet," said Max. "Let's get back down."

"Now you're cookin' with gas."

When Max got back to the main floor, he looked around some more, then went outside on the surrounding deck. Nothing there seemed amiss, so he went down the access stairs to the landing platform.

Standing on the platform's wooden planks, he could look up and see the wood framing under the floor of the lighthouse. Because of the hexagonal shape of the lighthouse's footprint, the floor framing was a series of wooden beams and steel girders. Aside from a few small bird's nests, nothing looked out of the ordinary. Max sighed and trudged up the stairs to the lighthouse.

Allison looked down at her notes and prepared to ask about the information she had gotten from Isis Dalrymple. Might as well let her have it all at once, she thought.

"Madame DeSousa", she began, "I understand your real name is Maude Flannagan and you used to work as a fortune teller at the Lowrey Brothers Circus."

Madame DeSousa looked startled for a second, then recovered. She smiled warmly.

"You know, you really must come to a séance, Allison. I think it would be so much more informative than a mere interview and a bunch of boring old trivial facts. You could actually see the spirits in action."

"See the spirits? That sounds intriguing. You mean blobs of ectoplasm drift about the room?"

"The spirits manifest themselves in a variety of ways, but I think I can guarantee you won't be disappointed. I have a séance scheduled for a week from Friday at 8 PM. Would you be able to attend?"

"And how! I'll be there with bells on."

Madame De Sousa smiled tolerantly. "That won't be necessary, my dear; the spirits will no doubt provide all the background noises you could wish for."

Allison decided to hold the more probing questions until after the séance. She thanked Madame DeSousa and strolled down Goldsborough Street to Harrison, then over to Dover Street to the rambling wood-shingled Avon Hotel.

Off the main lobby was an informal dining room. Allison sat at a table by the window and ordered a cup of tea and some toast. She spread her notes on the table and started going over them, making a correction or addition here and there.

"Why, hello Allison. What are you doing here?"

Allison looked up and saw Mabel Johnson, a neighbor from St Michaels. Mabel, who worked at the cannery in season, was short and pudgy, and favored drab clothes.

"I saw you through the window, and just had to stop by and say hello," she continued.

"Hello, Mabel. I'm just here researching my next article. What brings you up to Easton?"

Mabel sat down and sighed. "Oh, I have an appointment with Madame DeSousa."

"You go to Madame DeSousa? Whatever for?"

Mabel looked uncomfortable. "Just a little spiritual guidance. There's nothing wrong with that."

"Oh, I didn't mean there was anything wrong," said Allison. "I was just a little surprised, that's all. How long have you been going?"

"I started going when my Harold died last winter." She shook her head slowly and looked deeply sad.

"I told him it was too cold and stormy to go out tonging, but he said it was a good way to beat the others to the best oyster beds. He'd done it before; came home wet and half-frozen, but with 20 or 25 bushels of oysters. He always worked when the others stayed in. It helped to get us through many a winter. Then one day it was sleeting. Ice was everywhere. I told him not to go, but he wouldn't hear of it. The next day they found his boat and his tongs were still in it, along with 15 bushels of oysters, but Harold was gone. They said he must have slipped and fallen in that cold water."

Allison placed her hand on Mabel's shoulder. "I know, Mabel. It was a terrible thing."

Mabel took out a handkerchief and daubed her eyes. "Anyway, I come to see Madame DeSousa to contact Harold and tell him I'm all right. I increased my hours at the cannery cut back here and there, and took in a boarder, so I'm getting by."

Allison nodded in sympathy.

Mabel stood up suddenly and smiled. "Well, I must get going. I don't want to be late. Goodbye, Allison."

Allison watched her go out the door to Dover Street, then pulled out a copy of her notes and saw that Madame DeSousa charged two dollars for a session. Two dollars. That was a whole day's pay for Mabel at the cannery, a day's pay she could ill afford to lose, and all for some spiritual mumbo-jumbo. What kind of a person was Madame DeSousa, anyway?

Chapter 7

Suspicions

Around three o'clock, Sergeant Bentley returned to the Devil's Elbow light in a larger boat with three other men. They were up the stairs in a few seconds with a loud scrambling of footsteps.

"Well, I'm back," said Bentley, stating the obvious. "These boys are patrolmen with the department and this is the county coroner."

Three nondescript men dressed in dark suits nodded, then set off for the room with the lighthouse keeper's body.

"Anyone stop by while I was gone?" said Bentley.

"No," said Max, "but there is something unusual. There is what appears to be a brand new antenna wire up by the light."

Bentley shrugged. "And?"

"Nothing," said Max. "It just makes me wonder, that's all."

Bentley shook his head. "Now you're starting to make me wonder."

"I get that a lot."

In the next room, the coroner worked with the body for about a half hour, made a few notes, then took Max and Bentley aside.

"Fred, I have a problem here."

Bentley sighed. "Just one?"

"I've checked out the body from stem to stern and it looks like he died from a blow to the head."

"He wasn't stabbed?"

"Not a sign. No stab or bullet wounds, just a lot of bruises and abrasions plus one bashed in spot by his temple. What's more, I don't think the blood around here is his. There's no sign of anything on the victim that's been bleeding."

"Well, whose blood was it?"

"I'm just a medical man. I'll leave the detective work to you boys."

Bentley looked at Max.

"All right, Max. If you want to say I told you so, this is the time."

"Never mind that," said Max. "What happens now?"

"We take plenty of photos, then take the body back to Crisfield and station a deputy here until the Lighthouse Service can get a substitute out here. They've already been informed. They want to do their own investigation, but said we could take the body back to a funeral home once we took pictures."

A half hour later, the body was wrapped in a sheet and stowed aboard the Crisfield boat. Bentley paused at the head of the outside stairs and turned to Max, J.D, and Casper.

"I want to thank you boys for your help. I don't know what happened here, but I'm going to look into it. I suppose the Lighthouse Service will have someone investigating as well. Damndest thing I ever saw."

"Another boat seems to be approaching, Fred," said Max, shading his eyes. "This place is mighty popular all of a sudden."

They looked and saw a motor skiff heading for the light from the southeast, the direction of Crisfield. The occupant was a woman waving toward them.

"Well, I'll be," said Bentley. "That looks like Nell Paisley. "I wonder what she's doing way out here? Rumor has it that she and Jack Coleman were real close, if you know what I mean."

"I think we know," said Max.

"Boys," Bentley called to the coroner and the deputy in the boat below, "hold up a minute. Let's see what this lady wants."

A fortyish, dark haired woman wearing a dress that was more fit for a party than the Devil's Elbow pulled her boat up alongside the Karen Rebecca and called to Bentley.

"Sergeant Bentley, is it true? Did someone kill Jack...er...Mr. Coleman?"

"I'm afraid so, Nell. We're taking his body back now. I'm sorry."

"Wait there. I'm coming up."

Nell was out of her boat, across the Karen Rebecca, and up the stairs in a few movements. Up close, she was pleasant-looking in a dark, almost Spanish way. Her face was middle-aged and attractive, but lined with worry. She looked at Max and the watermen before speaking.

"Oh, this is Max Hurlock, J.D. Pratt and Casper Nowitsky. They're, ..er. ..helping me out. They're all right. Boys, this is Nell Paisley. Her husband owns the Paisley Club in town."

She hesitated a moment, then plunged ahead.

"Sergeant, when you investigated the scene, did you find his diary?"

Sergeant Bentley's eyes narrowed. "Diary? What makes you think he had a diary?"

"He used to come in the club. He mentioned it."

"I see. Well, we've been all over this place and there wasn't any diary. Maybe he kept it somewhere else. Why do you ask?"

"I want to see it before everyone else does, especially the newspapers."

"But why?"

"In case he wrote lies about me, that's why. He'd do that, you know. My husband threw him out of the club one night a few weeks ago and Jack Coleman said he'd have a lot of things to write down in his diary, things folks'd be interested to read. Well, I don't need no dead man slandering me, so I want that diary."

"Mrs. Paisley," said Sergeant Bentley patiently, "I'm afraid that diary, if it exists, will be part of the evidence in this case. If we found something like that, we couldn't hand it over to you or anyone else."

"Sergeant, that diary concerns me!"

"And murder concerns me. I have to hang onto any evidence I have. I'm sure you can appreciate that. Anyway, we're all just spittin' in the wind here because there is no diary, and I don't expect one will turn up. After all, we searched the place and he couldn't exactly bury it out in the yard, now could he?"

Nell Paisley was silent a moment, then spoke in a calmer voice. "All right, Sergeant, but would you at least tell me if any diary turns up?"

"Certainly. I'll be sure to tell you or Tom."

"No; not Tom! Please don't tell my husband."

"All right, all right; just you, then."

Nell nodded, went back to her boat and headed back toward Crisfield.

"Yet another interesting development," Max commented. "This case is full of them it seems."

Bentley shook his head. "How in tarnation could a man who lives in a lighthouse way out in the bay get himself so tangled up with folks in Crisfield?"

Max smiled. "I suppose that's what weekends are for. Well, Casper, J.D.; are you ready to head back up to Claiborne?"

"Hell yes, Max," said Casper. "I can't get out of this place soon enough."

Shadows were starting to lengthen as the Karen Rebecca retraced its earlier route back north up the bay. The rise and fall of the boat in the swell was almost hypnotic as the water churned by under the keel. The Karen Rebecca was opposite Taylors Island just south of the Choptank River when a gray patrol boat appeared off the port quarter.

"Is that the state oyster police?" Max asked.

J.D. looked back at the fast approaching boat.

"Not this time of year very much. Mid-winter is the big arster season. That's when the state boys'll be nosin' around to make sure everybody's playin' by the rules and nobody's drudgin' under power."

"Yeah, and to chase away any of those Virginia boys tryin' to scrape our arster beds," Casper added.

"Then who is it?" asked Max.

"Coast Guard, most likely," said J.D. "They're lookin' for rum runners."

It was true. Max could now make out the white letters CG-182 on the side of the hull.

"Yeah, that's one of them new six-bitters," No Whiskey observed. "They call 'em that because they're 75 feet long; just the thing for chasin' rum runners."

As if to confirm his conclusion a siren sounded.

"Ahoy," came a voice over a megaphone. "This is the Coast Guard. Heave to for inspection."

Casper cut the engine and the Karen Rebecca slowed and wallowed lazily in the water. The sleek gray form of the cutter pulled alongside, its wake rocking the Karen Rebecca. When the CG-182 was just a foot away, two men in blue uniforms stepped onto the deck of the Karen Rebecca. The CG-182 backed away slightly and stood off while the inspection was underway, a precaution against being boarded themselves.

"Afternoon," said the taller one, whose chevrons and hat identified him as a Master Chief Petty Officer, "Do you have any contraband on board?"

"Just Max here," said J.D.

The chief looked at Max, but said nothing. "Well, we'll just have a look around, then you can be on your way. Did you happen to pass by Devil's Elbow light?"

"We just came from there," said Max.

"Then you know about the light keeper."

"We sure do," said J.D. "We discovered the body."

The chief's eyebrows raised slightly. "Is that so? What happened?"

J.D. and Casper eagerly retold the events of the last two days. The chief listened intently and asked a few questions. He seemed outgoing and sympathetic, the kind of person you'd like to have a beer with.

"You boys have had a time of it. Any idea what happened to the light keeper?"

Casper and J.D. speculated on murder by rumrunners, Virginia dredgers, and even rival lighthouse keepers. While this conversation was going on, another Coast Guard man was examining the Karen Rebecca, paying particular attention to the bilge. Finally, Max spoke.

"Is the Coast Guard investigating the Devil's Elbow case, chief?"

"Not officially. That's in the bailiwick of the Lighthouse Service and maybe the locals, but naturally we're interested in maintaining navigation aids and we're patrolling the area all the time, so we've been asked to keep our eyes and ears open."

Max nodded. "Very sensible. Have you encountered any suspicious vessels in the area over the past few weeks?"

The chief pushed his hat back on his head. "Say, they're the only kind we do encounter sometimes; especially at night. That's when the rumrunners really come out. Lately we've been chasing this runner that looks like a modified work boat. You know; the kind they call a deadrise. She's maybe a 45 footer and runs at night with no lights. The damnedest thing is that this boat seems to be able to vanish. We almost had her two nights ago. We were hot on her tail and suddenly there was a flash of light and the boat disappeared. It just wasn't there anymore. We ran flat out for a few minutes, but there was no sign of her."

"No worry about that with this boat at least," Max observed, "so what is your partner looking for?"

"Booze, mostly," the chief replied.

"On an old workboat?"

The chief chuckled. "Oh yes. Some of these good ol' boys like to supplement their income with a little rum running now and again. A boat like this doesn't need to be fast as long as it's sneaky. Why just last week we stopped a bugeye and found she had a false bottom built into her. You lift up a few floorboards and you have room for at least fifty cases between the lower deck and the bilge."

"It seems a lot of ingenuity is going into getting around Prohibition," Max observed.

"Well, we have some ingenuity on our side, too."

The other Coast Guard man reappeared. "She's clean, chief."

The chief nodded, pulled out a logbook and entered the time, position, and name of the Karen Rebecca.

"Now if I could trouble you for your names and addresses, I think we can be on our way."

A few minutes later the two Coast Guardsmen stepped back onto the CG-182 and it roared away in a rumbling cloud of spray and foam.

"A right nice fella," J.D. observed.

"Salt of the earth," Casper added.

"They got a tough job," J.D. added.

"Dang near impossible, I'd say," said Casper.

Max shook his head. "For Pete's sake. Are you guys blind? Don't you know what he was doing?"

"What do you mean, Max?"

"He was coaxing you to keep talking and he was taking notes about everything you guys were so eagerly telling him; finding the body, stopping at the light yesterday, knowing Jack Coleman, and your wild speculations about what happened. Now the Coast Guard probably thinks you're suspects!"

"But we were just..."

"You were practically bragging about how involved you are. I had to change the subject or you guys would be in irons the way you were going."

"He was really doing that? How do you know, Max?"

"Because it's the same method I often use when I'm investigating a case. You put the suspect at ease and then encourage them to talk into your sympathetic ear.

Apparently the chief is something of an investigator as well."

"Well, tarnation, Max, we were just..."

"Never mind. I doubt that anything will come of it, but you may get hauled in for more questioning and miss more days on the water."

"That's just what we don't need," said J.D. glumly.

John Reisinger

Chapter 8

Down the shore

"Dead? The lighthouse keeper was dead?" Allison's eyes went wide when Max told her the news. "Oh, Max; how horrible. No wonder J.D. and Casper were nervous. Do they know who did it?"

"No. I'm afraid Sergeant Bentley and the Lighthouse Service have a mystery on their hands. Well, they can have it."

"Do you think you'll be asked to help?"

"Nix. There are two agencies on it already. The last thing they need is some nosey amateur gumming up the works. Besides, I don't have a client."

"Another quiet week on the Eastern Shore, I suppose."

"Speaking of the departed, how was your visit to Madame DeSousa?"

"Interesting. I got some background information on her from Isis Dalryple before I left."

"And did you expose her with the information you got from Isis Dalrymple?"

"No. I mentioned her real name and how she used to be a fortune teller in a circus. She changed the subject rather abruptly and invited me to her next séance. I figured I couldn't pass up an opportunity like that so I didn't press her on the other stuff."

"Ah. A tactical retreat in pursuit of a strategic victory later. Good thinking. So did she tell you anything spooky?"

"As a matter of fact, she did. She went all glassy eyed and told me you'd soon have a new case to solve and that I would be involved in it."

"Looks like the spirits struck out on that one."

"So it appears. Still, she put on a good act."

"Act is the right word."

"Max, you know Mabel Johnson in town?"

"Sure. She works at the cannery. Her husband Harold was lost on the ice last winter. A sad story."

"Well, it's even sadder than you know. I ran into her at the Avon Hotel. It seems she's been going to Madame DeSousa."

"Seems harmless enough."

"Harmless? Madame DeSousa charges two dollars for a session and Mabel has been going to her since her husband died. She's barely scraping by as it is and Madame DeSousa is squeezing what little money she has."

Max frowned. "That does sound bad. The more I hear about your Madame DeSousa the less I like her. Maybe you'll be doing a public service by exposing her."

"Yes, I'll be at that séance with my eyes wide open."

"Meanwhile, I have a building to check in Ocean City next week. What do you say we fly there? Gypsy could use the exercise since flying jobs have been a bit sparse."

"Gypsy's been acting a bit cranky lately. Couldn't we just take the 'Black Cinders and Ashes'? At least we'd be sure to get there."

"I'm impressed," said Max. "You're picking up the local dialect splendidly. Only a dyed in the wool Eastern Shore person would know to refer to the Baltimore Chesapeake and Atlantic Railroad's Ocean City Flyer that way. That train may be the most reliable way to get from Claiborne to Ocean City, but an airplane is faster and the view is better. I'll tell you what. We'll fly in Gypsy, but follow the rails to Ocean City."

"Oh, joy."

A few days later, Max and Allison flew their war surplus Curtiss Jenny biplane to Ocean City. As Max had promised, the view of the farmlands and the Delmarva Peninsula were breathtaking. At one point they passed over the Ocean City Flyer train chugging along and leaving a long trail of smoke in its wake. In an hour they were over a long sand bar along the Atlantic with white breakers surging against a white sand beach. Wood frame buildings clustered along a boardwalk filled with strollers as sunlight glinted off the waves that stretched to the far horizon.

They landed just outside of Ocean City and booked a room at the Atlantic Hotel on the boardwalk. At breakfast the next morning, someone had left a copy of the Baltimore Morning Sun on the table and they saw a front page article about the mysterious death of the lighthouse keeper. The article, which was two days old, went on to say that the Lighthouse Service had asked the Bureau of Investigation to take on the case.

"See?" said Max. "What did I tell you? They have it under control. I wish the B.I. the best of luck."

"I guess Madame DeSousa was wrong."

"Life is full of surprises. I have a meeting at 10:00, then we can walk on the beach."

After breakfast, Max went to his meeting and Allison strolled on the boardwalk. As she stood looking out to sea, and admiring the way the sun sparkled on the water, she was aware of a man looking the same way with a long telescope. He was elderly, with wispy white hair and the look of a slightly eccentric retired professor.

"There they are," he said. "I can see them as plain as day." He suddenly became aware that Allison was looking at him curiously, and looked slightly embarrassed.

"Pirates ships on the horizon?" Allison asked, smiling.

"In a manner of speaking, yes," the man replied. "Here, Miss. Look for yourself. You can't see it every day, but it's very clear this morning." He handed her the telescope and pointed to the horizon.

"I see two…no, three ships way out there," said Allison, wondering why ships on the ocean should arouse such an interest. "Are you saying they're pirates of some sort?"

"What you are looking at, young lady is part of Rum Row, the place just beyond the three mile American territorial limit where foreign liquor boats wait for nightfall to smuggle booze ashore. And that's just some of them; there's more off the Virginia Capes and the mouth of the Chesapeake."

Allison looked at him. "You mean they're rumrunners?"

The man shook his head. "No, they're the supply ships, the rumrunners are smaller, faster boats that unload the rum ships and sneak the liquor ashore. The Coast Guard and the Prohibition Police keep an eye on the rum fleet, but they can't be everywhere, and the rum boats can just sit and wait for a day or two if the law comes sniffing around."

"It sounds pretty brazen."

"Believe me, it's worth it. Just one of those ships can carry several million dollars' worth of bootleg."

"Where do they get it?"

"Oh Canada, Cuba and the Caribbean mostly. Our breweries might be shut down, but the ones overseas are working nights to keep up with demand. It's a big business now, courtesy of Prohibition. It's madness, that's what it is. They try to get rid of booze and wind up with more booze, more money and more crime. And when there's that much money involved, people start fighting over it."

"You mean gangsters?"

"Yes, but small timers as well. If they see a threat to their fat new income, things can get nasty."

Allison looked again at the three tiny silhouettes on the horizon. They didn't look sinister.

Allison still had the Morning Sun newspaper tucked under her arm. The man noticed it and pointed to the article she had just read with Max. His finger shook as he talked.

"Now you take that lighthouse keeper that was murdered; the one the papers are talking about. As sure as God made little green apples that man was killed by some rumrunner trying to keep his comings and goings a secret. A lighthouse keeper can see who's running and maybe he was reporting them. I wouldn't be surprised if some of the product from those very ships you're looking at was being run across the Chesapeake Bay to speakeasies in Baltimore, Annapolis and Washington. You want to know who killed the lighthouse keeper? Just look through that telescope!"

Max and Allison stayed another night, then returned to St Michaels that next afternoon. The weather had turned overcast with the threat of thunderstorms, a prospect that Allison didn't like one bit. But Gypsy performed well enough and shortly before three they began the descent to the field by their house. A few bumps and Gypsy rolled to a stop just a few yards from the barn with the sign that said Hurlock's Flying Service. Max hopped out with an eye on the storm clouds.

"Let's get Gypsy in the barn before the storm hits."

"We'll give you a hand."

Max turned and was surprised to see Casper Nowitsky and J.D Pratt walking rapidly from the direction of the house. They got Gypsy into the barn and made it back to the house just as the first drops of rain fell. They stood on the porch watching sheets of rain pelting the yard and making the air cool and fresh.

"All right, boys. Don't keep me in suspense. I know you didn't come all this way just to help me put Gypsy in the barn. What is it; another dead light keeper?"

J.D. sat heavily in a wicker chair on the porch. "No, Max; it's the same one. They're looking for who killed Jack Coleman..."

"And they're looking at us!" Casper added.

Chapter 9

Suspects

"I told you boys you talked too much. Now you have them suspecting you. What happened?"

"The Lighthouse Service called in the Feds to investigate, seein' as how law enforcement isn't exactly their specialty. So it seems the head of the Bureau of Investigation, a fella named Burns, sent this agent name of Gaston Means to Crisfield to get to the bottom of things. He's been talking to the Coast Guard, Sergeant Bentley, and all our friends. Then he cornered us. Started talkin' about how we were at the lighthouse just before Jack was killed. He even found another waterman who said he saw us high tailin' it out of there the day we stopped by the light."

"Were you?"

"Well, hell yes. We were tryin' to get back before another storm hit."

"So now you think they suspect you both?"

"Sure looks that way," said Casper. "We really fell into this one, Max. What are we going to do?"

"Sounds like you've done plenty already," said Max. "Well, I don't think you have much to worry about. After all, you didn't do it."

"But they don't have anybody else to blame that we can see," said J.D. "So they're squeezin' us. One day they question No Whiskey and the next day they question me. Now they're talking about taking us to Baltimore for more questions. Max we can't afford all this. We're missing out on crabbing and tonging. If we can't get them to leave us alone, we'll starve this winter. We'll have to start rum running just to put food on the table."

"Maybe you should get a lawyer," Max suggested.

"We haven't got the money for that," said Casper. "What we need is you, Max."

"Me? I'm not a lawyer."

"Right now we need somebody to find out what's going on and who killed Jack Coleman. Then they'll leave us alone and we can get back to honest work."

"Let me get this straight," said Max. "You want me to investigate Coleman's death and find the killer so they won't blame you?"

"You have to, Max. Nobody else believes us."

"Look J.D., No Whiskey, I can't just go up against the Bureau of Investigation. That's a federal agency. I don't have any authority…"

"You didn't have any authority when you pulled me out of the water when we got caught in that storm back when we were kids neither," said J.D.

"And what about that time you came by and towed my old boat back to shore when the engine broke and it was getting dark. What kind of authority did you have then?" said Casper.

Max sighed. "Well, I suppose I could at least talk to Fred Bentley and this… what was his name … Gaston

Means. Maybe I can find out where they're going and what they've learned. Maybe it's not as bad as you think. But I can't promise anything."

"Thanks, Max," said J.D. He turned to Allison who had been listening quietly.

"Miss Allison, your husband is a good man. God bless you both."

"Now wait a minute," Max interrupted. "Don't expect me to do all the dirty work. I'll need you boys to pull an oar too."

"Sure, Max. What can we do?"

"Keep your eyes and ears open, especially in local speakeasies. Others might be as talkative as you've been. I also want you to make a list of Crisfield watermen who work the Devil's Elbow area. I especially want to know who runs 'shine in his spare time."

"Sure Max. Anything else?"

"Yes. For Pete's sake stop volunteering information to Mr. Means."

The rain stopped and J.D. and Casper left for Tilghman Island. Max and Allison sat on the front porch enjoying the sounds of water dripping from the trees. Allison could see that Max was brooding.

"I have to hand it to you, Max; you have such interesting friends."

"Hmmmph. That old Chinese curse about 'May you live in interesting times' might just as well be 'May you have interesting friends.' J.D. and Casper must be exaggerating. They can't possibly be suspects, not for just stopping by the lighthouse at the wrong time."

"You're probably right. Maybe you can be the voice of reason and help everyone put things in perspective. Of course, there won't bet any money in it."

"They're my friends. I have to help them, even if it's just to reassure them."

"Stout fellow. What was it Shakespeare said? 'Words are easy, like the wind, but faithful friends are hard to find.'"

"Maybe, but I prefer that French general who said 'I can protect myself from my enemies, but God save from my friends.'"

The next morning, Max gassed up Gypsy for a flight down to Crisfield.

"Have a good trip, Max. I wish I could go with you, but I don't want to miss that Madame DeSousa séance tomorrow night and I'm not convinced you'll be back in time."

"You might be right. Anyway, I called Sergeant Bentley last night and he agreed to meet me at a farm where I can land. He says Gaston Means from the Bureau of Investigation is still there. He's operating out of a room at the Commercial Hotel on Main Street. I'll try to be back in a day or two. I'll ring you up tonight. You be careful going up to Easton now."

"Aye, aye, skipper," said Allison, saluting.

Max and Allison embraced, then Max climbed into the cockpit and took off heading south.

From an airplane, the low lying land between St Michaels and Crisfield looked as if was fighting to stay above water, and in some ways, it was. In that relatively short distance, Max flew over several river mouths, numerous coves and inlets, vast areas of grassy marsh, and a dozen or more islands of all sizes. Several of those islands were slowly eroding and sinking in a protracted death spiral. Almost the entire population of Holland Island, not far from the lighthouse, had moved to the mainland to escape the rising water, taking whatever possessions or parts of their houses they could manage.

The waterfront town of Crisfield, however, was prospering. From the air, Max could see that Crisfield clung to the end of a peninsula jutting into Tangier Sound on the lower Chesapeake Bay. A railroad line split the town almost down the middle, and ended at the Steamship Dock. Canneries and packing houses were placed with the water on one side and the railroad on the other. The trains hauled carloads of canned oysters from canneries and packing houses along the tracks to customers and restaurants all over the world.

Max could see the huge mounds of oyster shells outside the packing houses and the workboats and buy boats lined up at the dock to sell their catch. Buy boats were middlemen, circulating among the watermen and buying their daily catch for resale to the packing houses. Although they paid less than the packing houses, they enabled the watermen to save the time it took to sell the catch to the packing houses themselves. Scores of other boats were in the approach channels, going to or from the hazy waters of the Chesapeake Bay beyond. Max could see the whole process below him; oysters hauled by boat to the packing houses, then shipped out by train, leaving only mountains of empty shells behind.

Max circled and spotted the farm Fred Bentley had told him about. The red barn was unmistakable. He brought Gypsy in for a smooth landing and taxied up to an automobile with a man standing next to it.

"Mornin' Max," said Bentley. "So this is your flying machine, is it?"

Sergeant Bentley looked critically at the struts and wires that stiffened and braced the wings, and shook his head. "Not sure I'd trust my life to that thing, but to each his own I suppose."

"She's pretty reliable," said Max, patting the fabric under the engine, "though she has been running rough lately. I may have to overhaul the engine."

Bentley just shook his head.

"Thanks for picking me up, Fred," said Max. "J.D. and No Whiskey are worried about the investigation and I thought I'd talk to you and get the straight story."

"Sure thing, Max. Hop in the old flivver here and we can talk on the way into town."

In a minute they were on the main road into town.

"Sorry it's a bit bumpy, Max, but the street's paved with oyster shells, so it's a mite rough at times. Matter of fact, the whole dang town is built on oyster shells, at least the part along the water front."

Max smiled. "I suppose they do pile up."

"Yeah. We have us a lime plant in town that grinds up a lot of the shells and makes lime for cement, but we still have tons of the things."

"Speaking of things that are hard and unwanted, what can you tell me about the investigation into the lighthouse keeper's murder?"

Bentley frowned in an annoyed way. "Damned feds. They just came in here and took over. Pretty much pushed me aside. I'm still looking into the case, but now they won't let me go back to the lighthouse. Well, I suppose it is their territory at that, but it sticks in my craw sometimes."

"So what's this Gaston Means like?"

"Means? I can't figure him out at all. He was hand-picked by Bill Burns himself. Burns is the head of the BI and used to be the head of the Burns Detective Agency. He's a good man as far as I know."

"But what about Means?"

"Maybe you should meet him yourself. He's got a room at the Hotel Commercial over on Main Street."

Death at the Lighthouse

"I'll stop by. Is it true he suspects J.D. and No Whiskey?"

"Can't say. But then he doesn't exactly confide in me. He looked at my report and the photos and the autopsy, and he's been talkin'..."

"There's been an autopsy report?"

"Just out late yesterday. I have a copy in my office. I just finished reading it before you got here."

"So what was the cause of death?"

"A blow to the head. Just like you thought."

"With what?"

"The doc wasn't sure, just that it was something blunt. Like a club or a brick or something. Whatever it was, it struck Coleman hard enough to crack his skull and kill him. The point is, someone else was there that night and got real physical with our friend Mr. Coleman. It was either an attack or a fight, but it was violent and the result was one dead lighthouse keeper."

Max digested this a moment.

"Of course the visitor could have attacked Coleman, but Coleman could just as well have attacked the visitor."

Sergeant Bentley looked thoughtful. "Yes, I suppose that's so."

"There was no other evidence found?"

"The autopsy didn't mention any, but Means would know better than I would at this point."

"What about the bloody footprint?"

"I looked at an enlargement of the photo. Near as I can tell, it was just a rubber work boot. Every waterman has at least one pair in these parts."

"And what about the new radio antenna?"

"Are you on about that dang radio again. Max? That was just a coincidence."

"When it comes to murder, I don't believe in coincidences."

"Well, there's nothin' so far about a radio."

"How about bootleggers? Have you got a lot in this area?"

Sergeant Bentley laughed. "That's like askin' if the packing plant has a lot of arster shells. Hell, you can hardly throw a brick without hittin' a bootlegger. Of course we had plenty of 'em even before Prohibition, but there's been what you might call an expansion since then. I could spend all my time chasin' 'em if I wanted to, and still not make a dent. I bust up several stills a week, but they build 'em faster than I can bust 'em."

"How about rumrunners?"

"The two go hand in hand. No sense makin' shine if you can't get it to the customers. Practically everybody with something that'll float gets in on the business once in a while; strictly amateur for the most part, but there's a few that are more professional about it. The Murphy boys, Brian and Patrick up on Jones Creek are probably the best. They have a fleet of local boys with speedboats, draketails, crab skiffs, deadrises, and I don't know what-all. They sort of coordinate the other runners. A bootlegger needs some product moved, he contacts one of the Murphys and they contact someone in their network. It's a pretty good system. If a runner gets caught, the Murphy boys are in the clear. Rumor has it that the Murphys have a couple of boats of their own for very special shipments they run personally, but I've never been able to confirm that."

"Any chance of my meeting the Murphys?"

"I doubt it. They don't talk to strangers unless the stranger is looking for some midnight shipping. That's how they keep out of jail. Brian Murphy usually comes to Crisfield for supplies at Tawes Hardware or Tull's

Grocery, or even Gordon's on Wednesdays, and that's tomorrow, but he'll probably keep to himself unless he knows you. Brian is the older brother, and as near as I can tell, the brains of the outfit. Patrick is more of a helper. Well, here we are at my office."

They had been traveling down Main Street, the central street with the railroad tracks in the center Max had spotted from the air. At the lower end of town, stores and packing plants lined the road on the harbor side and Max could make out patches of water and boats tied up at docks on the end of a number of side streets as they passed by. Barrels and crates of freshly canned oysters were stacked along the railroad tracks as men in boots and long aprons hauled them from the canneries and loaded them on to the waiting trains. Some dogs, cats, and even a few chickens seemed to have made themselves at home on the busy street as well, no doubt waiting for a handout, or a spill. Sergeant Bentley's Model T bumped down the street and splashed in several of the puddles that stood everywhere. The fishy smell grew stronger.

Bentley's office was a small room attached to a two cell jail, presently unoccupied, near the custom house almost at the very end. Bentley rode over several rail sidings as lines of freight cars slowly moved in the other direction. He pulled up in front of a one story brick building as several large freight cars squealed and clanked past. As far as Max could tell, the tracks went all the way to the end of the steamboat pier and ended in a large shed at the water's edge.

"The Crisfield Police headquarters is about a half mile farther north," Bentley explained, "but they keep this office here at the end of town to have a presence near the dock areas. Main Street veers off from the rail tracks about a half mile up the road from the steamboat

Pier and the bulk of the non-oystering part of town is located there, where the smell of the packing plants isn't as strong. So naturally, when they get some water crime, it usually falls on me."

Sergeant Bentley ushered Max into his office and sat behind an old desk. The usual small town police office décor was in place; tattered wanted posters on the walls, a bulletin board with notices and patrol schedules, a locked gun cabinet, a table with several mismatched chairs, some nondescript boxes here and there, and several ancient file cabinets. The view out the single window revealed the side of a box car on a siding. Bentley took the autopsy report out of a drawer and handed it to Max. Max read it and confirmed what Bentley had told him on the way into town.

"Fred, is it fair to say that whatever Means thinks, you don't consider J.D. and No Whiskey as suspects?"

"I can't say there's much evidence against those boys, but they were the last ones to see the victim alive that we know of, so I can't count them out just yet."

Max handed the autopsy report back to Sergeant Bentley.

"Fred, I suppose you patrol down here around the dock area and rail tracks at night?"

"Depends on what else is doin', but I try to take a swing by at least once or twice a night to make sure ain't nobody messin' with someone else's boat."

"Very commendable. On the night Jack Coleman was killed, did you notice any boats missing?"

Bentley shrugged. "There's always some boats missing, what with repairs, overnight trips, people getting back late, and what not. There's even a few old boat sheds where you can't tell if a boat is in 'em or not. Still, I don't recall anything that struck me as unusual, like a boat missing that was never missing before."

"Well, if you remember anything like that, I'd sure be interested to know. Say, do you have a copy of the photographs they took at the lighthouse?"

"Oh, sure thing." Sergeant Bentley opened a desk drawer and took out a stack of photos. "Here you go."

Max looked over the photos and didn't see anything much different than he remembered. Finally, he came to a picture of the footprint and an enlargement of that picture.

"Anything strike you as unusual about this boot print, Fred?" Max asked casually.

"The tread looks like the left foot of a standard Lambertville rubber boot," said Sergeant Bentley. "A lot of people have them."

Max was still looking intently at the photo.

"Maybe so, but how many people have this diagonal cut in the tread?"

"What? Let me see that. Well, I'll be damned. I believe you're right. Too bad we can't go around inspecting everyone's boot sole."

"Not everyone," said Max, "just one particular person."

The Commercial Hotel was a weathered wooden two story Victorian affair on a street corner well up Main Street from the dock area and across from the Lyric Theater. This part of Main Street was free of the industry and the railroad tracks in the lower part and had a decidedly less busy air about it. A brown mongrel dog snoozing on the porch of the hotel raised his head several inches when Max approached, decided it wasn't worth the effort, then went back to sleep.

The desk clerk told Max that Mr. Means had gone to the post office to make a call to his office in Washington and was expected back shortly. Max sat on the front porch and watched the meager activity along the street. At this hour of the day, most citizens of Crisfield were engaged in harvesting, shucking, or canning oysters. A few automobiles and horse-drawn wagons passed by, along with a few motor trucks.

Presently, Max noticed a portly, balding middle aged man walking down the street wearing a blue vested suit, a bow tie, and a fedora, and guessed this was Gaston Means. The man stepped on the porch and Max stood up.

"Mr. Means?"

The man stopped and looked Max over carefully. He had a curious alertness about him, like a man who was constantly on his guard and looking for opportunity. His expression and his mannerisms made him look as if he was trying to decide which of your pockets to pick first.

"Agent Gaston Means at your service," he replied finally with a slight bow.

"I'm Max Hurlock. I'm trying to gather some information about the death of the lighthouse keeper and wondered if I could speak to you for a moment."

"Hurlock? That name sounds familiar. Ah yes. You were with Mr. Pratt and Mr. Nowitsky when they discovered the body, were you not?"

"Yes, that's right."

"Are you acting as representative for these men?"

"I'm not an attorney, Mr. Means. I'm an investigator and a friend."

Means smiled wolfishly. "Splendid. You strike me as a man of culture and education Mr. Hurlock, a refreshing change from most of the people I've been dealing with here. I'm afraid I have no proper office in Crisfield, but the porch is commodious and reasonably private except for the occasional passer-by. We can talk here."

"Fine. I've talked to the Crisfield Police and seen the autopsy report and I'd be interested to know how your investigation is proceeding."

"Wait a minute," said Means suddenly. "Now I know where else I have come across your name. You solved that double murder up in New Jersey didn't you?"

"Yes, that was me, but..."

"And that puzzling poisoning case down in Georgia if I recall. Splendid work, Mr. Hurlock. As a brother investigator, I salute you."

"Well.."

"So I feel compelled to be completely candid with you in a way I never could be with a member of the general public."

"I appreciate that."

Means dropped his voice and sounded as if he were relaying a secret. "Oh, this is a complex business, Mr. Hurlock. Deep and troubling. There are wheels within wheels."

"Meaning what?"

Means was quiet a moment as someone came out of the hotel, then paused to light a cigarette before proceeding down the street. Once the man was on his way, Means continued.

"As an investigator I must go where the evidence leads, no matter how painful. I'm sure you can understand that."

"Of course. I do the same thing."

"Well, at the moment we have a man who is dead at the hands of someone else, and we have only two people who were seen at the lighthouse just before it happened."

"Wait a minute," Max protested. "It was at least another 12 hours, most of them in darkness, before the body was found. A lot could have happened in that time and no one would have seen it."

Means held up a hand. "Of course, and that could well be what occurred. The problem is that there is no evidence other than the sighting of your two friends the day before. We also know that they were both acquainted with Mr. Coleman, so much so that they could drop by unannounced. Who knows what else transpired between them; money owed, a disagreement over a card game, women. It could be anything."

"And it could be nothing," Max reminded him. "The courts generally expect evidence before convicting anyone. They're funny that way."

Means shrugged. "Oh, I know the case is somewhat circumstantial at the moment, but who knows what might turn up? Meanwhile, I must continue my investigation. I probably won't have a warrant for their arrest for at least another week or two."

Max rose from his chair. "Then I'm sure you wouldn't mind if I do a little investigating on my own."

Means looked up and smiled. "Excellent! I would consider it an honor. Of course you will keep me informed of your progress?"

"Oh, you'll be among the first to know."

"Wonderful, but there is something you should know, if you would be seated so I don't have to say it too loudly..."

Max sat back down and Means leaned toward him.

"This is highly confidential, but I think that as a fellow investigator, you have the right to know everything I do."

"Go on."

"Just two days ago I was approached by a man who claimed he knew who was really responsible for this crime. This man calls himself John Smith, though I'm certain that's an alias. He claims he lives next to an office in Salisbury that is being used as a meeting place for a bootlegging consortium. He overheard them talking about a lighthouse keeper that needed to be 'taken care of'. He was curious, so he began to spend a lot of time outside tending to his shrubbery so he could get closer."

"He had a good angle to see through a window, and he noticed that at the end of each meeting the gang would gather whatever papers they had and place them in a metal box they would then lock and place in a closet that was also locked. Once they met at night and he could see into the lighted room very well. He tells me that the metal box contains papers, notes, ledgers, accounting books, and even what appears to be a diary. He is convinced that this information would prove that the consortium killed Coleman."

"Great," said Max. "Then get a court order and raid the place."

"Alas, if only it were that simple," said Means, with a pained expression. "Mr. Smith has refused to divulge the location, or even his real name. He has promised to contact me again, but he is afraid of retaliation and wants to stay out of sight."

"So where does that leave us?"

"He has agreed to meet me here tonight, so we shall see if he is ready to provide more useful details. Why don't you stop by tomorrow around this time and we'll see where we are."

Max looked at his pocket watch. "I'll be back around noon tomorrow."

After leaving Gaston Means, Max returned to Sergeant Bentley's office on the waterfront. Bentley was glad to see him.

"Ah, Max. Did you get the word from our Mr. Gaston Means?"

Max sat down in an old wooden chair with one arm missing. "I got quite a few words from Mr. Means. Making sense of them, however, is another matter."

Bentley nodded. "Yes, that old boy sure does like the sound of his own voice. Mercy!"

"He seems to have J.D. and No Whiskey in his sights by default. He can't turn up any better suspects, although I don't know how hard he's trying. Did he tell you about the mysterious informant?"

Bentley leaned forward in his chair.

"Informant? He has an informant?"

Max told him about Means's tale of Mr. Smith and the box full of incriminating documents.

"Well, dang! Why am I the last to know? Didn't he think that little fact might be of some interest to me?"

"I have an idea why he told me, but I'm keeping an open mind for the moment," Max replied. "How did you size up Mr. Means?"

Sergeant Bentley shrugged. "Not for me to say. I'm not in charge. I'm just the fella the town hires to break up bar fights, make the drunks go home, and smash a still now and again. That lighthouse ain't even in my jurisdiction. Means represents the feds so he's got the whip hand in this case. 'Bout all I can do is watch and gripe once in a while."

"Don't sell yourself short, Fred. I suspect you can see and hear a lot, even if you're not running the investigation. And the first thing I want to know is your impression of Means."

Bentley looked around as if afraid of being overheard, then lowered his voice.

"He may be a bona fide agent for the U.S. Bureau of Investigation, and the apple of old Bill Burns's eye, but that man strikes me as a grifter in a ten dollar suit."

After leaving Sergeant Bentley, Max strolled along the docks and talked to some watermen and cannery workers about the death of the lighthouse keeper and who was out on the water the night it happened.

Other than a few modest church steeples scattered around the skyline and some tomato canneries, almost everything in Crisfield seemed to exist to serve the oyster industry. At the water's edge, the air was thick with a fishy smell and the piers by the canneries were crammed with buy boats that bought the day's catch directly from watermen out on the bay, took a cut for themselves, then sold the cargo to the packing houses ashore. Some watermen preferred the higher prices but lower convenience of selling directly to the packing plants, so there was also a selection of white-painted workboats of every description; two masted pungies, stately skipjacks with their sails furled, sleek crab skiffs, and smaller boats all selling baskets of freshly harvested oysters to the packing plants. Piles of discarded oyster shells rose as tall as the buildings, and men in tall rubber work boots, aprons and gloves hauled dripping baskets from the boats into the canneries constantly. Through the noise and chaos, Max was able to talk to several of the watermen. Everyone had the same story.

"I came in around dinner time," one said. "I was afraid that storm was coming back so it wasn't worth it.

Fact is, I don't know nobody as was out that night... 'cept maybe the rumrunners."

Everyone seemed to have a theory. As Max talked to the watermen, then to people from the packing plant as they left at the end of the day, he heard the killing blamed on everyone from rumrunners to other lighthouse keepers, to some shady criminal gang, to the thieving Virginia oystermen poaching on Maryland oyster beds. One imaginative soul was convinced the guilty party was his "no-good brother in law".

One cannery worker, however, seemed to have a different view. He noticed Max talking to people and came over to investigate.

"I wouldn't listen to all the rumrunner talk, mister," he said, finally.

Max turned to him. The man offered his hand.

"Tawes is the name; John Millard Tawes. My family owns a lot of business property in this town and we know the place pretty well."

Max shook his hand. "I'm Max Hurlock. Glad to meet you. So what do you hear, Mr. Tawes?"

As Tawes spoke, he was constantly interrupted by passers-by greeting him. He seemed to know everyone in Crisfield.

"Well, Prohibition's been around for four years now and there's never been any trouble at the light before, not even a rumor. My guess is that either the murder was for something personal, or that something changed in the status quo."

"The status quo?"

"Almost everyone around here knows of someone mixed up in bootlegging in some way, but they don't usually turn 'em in to the law. It's sort of live and let live. Otherwise, everybody'd be looking over his shoulder and suspicious of his neighbor all the time and that's no way to live."

Max nodded. "So when you say there might have been a change in the status quo, you mean…"

"Something changed and the apple cart got upset. Something changed the rules all of a sudden. You find out what that was and you'll find your killer."

After a quick dinner at a crab place up the street, Max strolled around the streets again and finally returned to the Hotel Continental just as it was getting dark. The desk clerk let him use the telephone and he placed a call to Allison to wish her luck at the séance.

"I'm all set, Max. I'm wearing my dark blue dress and a matching hat. I think it lends a proper air of solemnity to the occasion. I was all decked out in that yellow print number at first. It looked pretty good, but then I thought it might look too festive. I wouldn't want the spirits to think I'm not taking them seriously, or that I'm not sympathetic. It's so hard to know the proper protocol when meeting the dead."

"I'm having a similar problem down here," said Max.

"So did anyone confess yet?"

"No, but I had an interesting conversation with the agent from the Bureau of Investigation, Gaston Means. He claims someone has offered to spill the beans on the real killers."

"Really? Why that's marvelous. Who is this paragon of civic virtue?"

"That's the problem. Means says he doesn't know the man's real identity, and the man is being somewhat hesitant about producing the necessary evidence."

"Rats. So I guess that leaves you behind the eight ball."

"Not entirely, Allison. I have a few thoughts of my own about Mr. Means and his reluctant stool pigeon. I'll let you know more tomorrow. Oh, by the way, if Madame DeSousa summons up the spirit of Jack Coleman, be sure to ask him what happened. It would save a lot of trouble."

Max hung the phone and looked around the lobby. The desk clerk asked him if he was going up to his room.

"Not just yet," he replied, looking around and taking a deep breath. "It looks like a nice night for a stroll."

With that, Max was out the front door. The clerk watched him as he disappeared into the darkness down the street.

Chapter 10

The spirits come to call

With the darkness outside, the thick curtains and tapestries, the heavy furniture and the dim lighting, Madame DeSousa's parlor looked like just the sort of place spirits might prefer to patronize. Several other guests were already seated and sipping glasses of red pseudo wine Madame DeSousa had thoughtfully provided. Madame DeSousa's had not yet appeared, but a drab looking male assistant greeted the guests.

"Good evening, Mrs. Hurlock. Please have a seat and a glass of our wine. May I introduce your fellow guests? This is Mrs. Culhane. Mrs. Flagler, Mrs. Quincy, Mr. Davis, and Mr. St John. Ladies and gentlemen, this is Mrs. Hurlock. When you have finished your wine, please take your seats around the table. Madame DeSousa will be among you in a few moments."

The guests greeted Allison, drained their glasses and found places around the table with an air of nervous excitement. Allison took the seat next to where Madame DeSousa would sit so she could observe closely.

"Isn't this exciting?" said Mrs. Flagler, in a hushed, reverential tone. "I can almost feel the spirits already!"

"Well, we will see," said Mr. St John. "But you never know."

"Have you been to a séance before?" Mrs. Culhane asked to no one in particular. Everyone except Allison nodded their heads.

"You've never been to a séance, my dear?" said Mrs. Quincy. "Oh, you are in for a real experience. The cat's pajama's, as I believe is the current expression."

"I'm sure it will be darb," said Allison.

"I just adore Madame DeSousa," said Mrs. Flagler. The others nodded solemnly.

The lights dimmed even more, plunging the room into almost complete darkness. Only the faint glow of a small lamp in the middle of the table provided any illumination. As everyone's eyes were straining to adjust to the darkness, they heard a voice.

"Good evening everyone. I am Madame DeSousa and I welcome you."

The light in the middle of the table brightened and Allison was startled to see Madame DeSousa apparently materialize in the chair opposite. Where did she come from? Madame DeSousa was dressed in a black medieval-looking gown with long loose sleeves and what looked like a cloak with a hood. The guests breathed a collective ahhh, then fell silent, awaiting some solemn pronouncement from their host.

Madame DeSousa did not disappoint.

"Tonight I will attempt to contact my spirit guide, and through him to communicate with certain of the departed, those who have passed over to the world of the spirits. The spirits may manifest themselves in a physical way tonight. You must not be frightened. They will not harm you."

That's a relief, Allison thought.

"Sometimes our guests include those who are skeptical, who are not sure about the spirit world."

Allison could have sworn everyone was looking at her.

"Such people are welcome as long as they maintain the proper decorum. So there will be no question about the origin of what you may see or hear, I would ask that you hold the hand of the person on each side of you and place your foot in contact with that person's foot as well. That way there will be no possibility of anyone, myself included, manipulating any devices or tricks. To make absolutely sure, I would ask those on either side of me to place their foot over the toe of my shoe and to keep them there."

Allison complied. She grasped Madame DeSousa's hand and slid her foot over the toe of her shoe.

Now let her try some funny business, she thought. Allison looked around and saw the assistant was also seated at the table. Now the light got even dimmer again and the room was in almost complete darkness. Allison frowned. With everyone sitting around the table and holding hands, she wondered just who had dimmed the light.

"I must have complete silence as I try to contact my spirit guide," said Madame DeSousa.

For a minute, all was quiet as Madame DeSousa rocked slightly in her chair and moaned faintly. Allison grasped her hand and pressed down on her foot.

"If you can hear me, please make your presence known. Give us some sign, so that we may know."

From somewhere close by came the faint sound of a bell. Allison looked around and saw nothing. The bell repeated, louder this time. Something caught the corner of Allison's eye; she looked around and saw floating in the darkness above their heads, a faintly glowing bell.

"Holy cats," she whispered.

The bell circled the group then disappeared, but now the table started moving, rising and falling like some living thing. Now a bugle appeared overhead, drifting and softly glowing in the darkness. At this point, Allison was sorry Max would not be home when she tried to sleep later.

"My spirit guide has brought the spirit of Mrs. Quigley's dear deceased mother Ida."

Somewhere in the darkness, Allison heard Mrs. Quigley gasp.

"She wants Mrs. Quigley to know she is happy and that she is watching over her and her family."

"Tell her I'm sorry I was cross with her just before she died," said Mrs. Quigley. "I've felt terrible about it ever since."

"Ida Quigley says she forgives you and loves you very much," said Madame DeSousa. "She is in a better place and is serene and content. She wishes you a long and happy life and looks forward to seeing you again someday when you too pass over."

In the darkness, Mrs. Quigley softly wept.

Now it was Mr. St John's turn. Madame DeSousa summoned his late wife, who arrived with the sound of a violin softly droning in the darkness. Allison looked around expecting to see a violin, but saw something wispy and gauze-like floating above them and lazily drifting.

"Jeepers," Allison whispered wide eyed. "What is that?"

Mr. St John's wife assured him she was nearby and stroked him on the back of the head with an invisible hand. He almost fainted.

After a few more manifestations of this sort, Madame DeSousa gave the spirits permission to depart, which they did with a noticeable gust of air that had the subjects almost jumping out of their seats. Madame DeSousa told everyone to release each other's hands and the lights came back up. Everyone remained frozen in place for a few moments as the assistant rose from the table to help Madame DeSousa to a back room to recover from her exhausting ordeal.

"Whew!" said Allison, breaking the silence. "So that's a séance."

The guests compared impressions in hushed tones; as if afraid the spirits might hear them and take offense.

"Are you all right, dear?" said Mrs. Culhane. "You look a bit unsteady on your feet."

"I'm a little overwhelmed," Allison replied. "My head feels like the spirits wacked me with a sock full of doorknobs."

"I felt that way at my first séance as well. My knees were shaking and my mouth was too dry to speak. The spirits can come on a bit strong, but that's part of the experience."

Madame DeSousa reentered the room. She looked tired, but alert.

"Well, did the spirits appear?"

"You didn't notice?" Allison was amazed anyone could have overlooked the ghostly chaos of the previous half-hour.

"Oh, no," Madame DeSousa smiled. "When I go into a spiritual trance, I become completely unaware of my surroundings. The spirits take over."

"The spirits did appear," said Mr. St John. "It was magnificent."

Madame DeSousa smiled. "I am so glad." She looked at Allison.

"Was the experience what you expected, Allison?"

"I have to admit," said Allison, "it was more than I expected. I'll have to think about it."

"Fair enough."

"I think I saw some sort of white gauze floating around."

Madame DeSousa nodded. "Ectoplasm, no doubt. It's a spiritual energy the medium produces that enables the spirits to interact in our world. It's generated by the ectenic or psychic force within the human body."

"Oh. Well, that explains it."

Madame DeSousa grasped Allison's hands. "I'm so glad you could come tonight, Allison, I really…"

"Yes?"

Madame DeSousa was staring at Allison as if seeing her for the first time. She looked disoriented and confused.

"Are you all right?"

Madame DeSousa was trembling slightly.

"Allison. You must tell your husband to look for the mermaid."

"Look for the mermaid? What mermaid? What do you mean?"

Madame DeSousa shook her head as if to clear away the thoughts. She looked at Allison again.

"I…I don't know. I just had a vision of a mermaid. I'm as much in the dark as you are."

Allison looked around nervously. She would be glad to get home and lock the door behind her.

The road back to St Michaels seemed much longer, darker, and more twisted than Allison remembered it. The trees in the deep black shadows by the side of the road seemed to be restless and reaching out for her, and she could have sworn the moon was following her. When she finally got home she locked the door behind her and looked under the beds carefully.

John Reisinger

Chapter 11

Deals

The next morning in Crisfield, Max was out early and walked around the dock area before he went to the Paisley Club to talk with Nell Paisley.

The throngs of workboats were mostly gone at this hour, on their way to oyster beds along the bay, but the waterfront was still buzzing with activity. The shuckers at the packing houses had started work around five AM, shucking the remaining oysters brought in the day before to be ready for this day's catch that would start arriving around noon. The last freight train from the day before was gone and the next one was just arriving, slowly backing down the street with a chorus of thumps and metallic clanking.

Almost every business Max saw along the waterfront seemed to be related to oystering in some way, and the few that weren't sold groceries or farm supplies. A few stray watermen in rubber boots walked about on various missions, and the place had a busy small town look to it.

Max was passing by the Crisfield Mercantile Company and wondering how Allison had done at the séance last night when he heard someone call his name.

"Hey, Max. Is that you?"

He turned and was surprised to see Duffy Merkle emerging from the store. Merkle was a St Michaels moonshiner Max had known for years, but had never turned in, since Max was not a law enforcement official.

"Hey, Duffy," said Max. "How's the liquid refreshment business?"

Duffy, a squat bearded man in faded overalls laughed. "My moonshine is going great, Max. In fact I'm just down here discussing deliveries with my distributer."

"How did you do with the Prohibition police? I heard they smelled the corn mash and tracked it to your place."

"Aw, that was nothin'. I just dumped the mash in with the pigs and nobody was the wiser. Just a cost of doin' business you might say. So what brings you to Crisfield?"

"I'm checking up on the death of the Devil's Elbow light keeper for J.D. Pratt and No Whiskey. They're afraid they're going to get blamed since they were at the light just before the keeper was killed."

"Another danged murder! I figured you'd get pulled into that one."

"Hey Duffy. You ready to go?" a voice called from the door of a shop."

"Sure thing. Hey, come on over here. I want you to meet someone."

Another man was just emerging from the store. He was medium height and wiry. He had thinning blond hair and a scraggly mustache, and wore a coarse brown suit.

"Brian, This here's my pal Max Hurlock. He's the best dang detective you ever seen. Max, this is my business associate, Brian Murphy."

"Brian Murphy?" said Max. "Of the Jones Creek Murphys?"

Brian Murphy nodded, but looked wary.

"Listen," said Max, "have you boys had breakfast yet? It's on me. I'd really like to talk to you."

Murphy hesitated, but Duffy Merkle came to the rescue.

"Shoot, Brian. You don't have to worry about Max, here. I've known him for years and he's a straight shooter. Hell, if he was inclined to tell secrets, I'd a been in jail long ago."

"You said he was a detective," said Murphy. His eyes shifted from side to side as if afraid of being watched.

"I'm an independent investigator," said Max, "but I'm not connected with the police or any law enforcement organization. I do not enforce the Prohibition laws, so unless you're planning a murder, anything you say is safe with me."

Murphy still hesitated.

"Look," said Max. "I'm investigating the death of Jack Coleman so a couple of waterman friends of mine don't get sent up the river for it."

"What friends?" said Murphy, still with no expression.

"J.D. Pratt and Casper Nowitsky."

"Five by Five and No Whiskey? Someone's looking to pin the blame on them? All right. I believe maybe I'll have some bacon and eggs after all."

Betty's Eatery a few doors away was a dingy place that smelled of fried foods and featured greasy looking tables and coils of flypaper hanging from the ceiling.

When the three had settled into a table in the corner, Max got down to business.

"Look, Mr. Murphy..."

"You can call me Brian. After all, you know Five by Five and No Whiskey."

"All right, Brian. I know about your business. I have no interest in interfering in any way, and anything I could tell the authorities they probably already know, but you have your finger on the pulse of most of the running that's going on around here and I need to know about Jake Coleman and how he was involved. If he was involved, that is. Some people are saying that Coleman was killed by bootleggers to keep him quiet. Some people say he was watching the rumrunners and reporting them to the Coast Guard."

Brian Murphy chewed a forkful of scrambled eggs. "Some people don't know what the hell they're talking about."

"So he wasn't killed by bootleggers?"

Murphy swallowed his eggs and looked at Max as if sizing him up. Finally, Murphy spoke quietly. "Look, Max. Rum running's a business, just like any other."

"Ceptin' it's illegal," Duffy chimed in.

"Right, but legal or not, the last thing any business needs is something disrupting operations; especially if that something involves the police. Now I'm not admitting anything, mind you, but some of my associates are afraid to go out on the water at night around that area now because they figure the police or the Coast Guard will be on the alert. So I've got fewer runners to use and lower delivery capacity to offer. That murder has been bad for business. For anybody runnin' 'shine, this hornet's nest is the last thing they need."

"But what if Coleman had been observing the runners and reporting, or threatening to report them to the police the way some people say? Wouldn't that make someone want him out of the way?"

Brian Murphy took another forkful of eggs and looked around before continuing. "Look. Here's how it is. On any given night there must be at least 30 to 50 runners in the lower bay and just as many from the Choptank north. Some carry liquor from the Eastern Shore over to Virginia, Southern Maryland, and Washington up the Patuxent and the Potomac, and some carry liquor the other direction."

"Wait," said Max. "Rum running goes in both directions across the bay? Why?"

Murphy shrugged. "I told you it was a business and a business has to satisfy its customers. Some folks on the west side have a taste for Eastern Shore corn liquor and some folks over here prefer the stuff brewed on the west side. Anyway, in addition to this two way running, there's boats that run out to the bay empty and unload ships from the rum fleet offshore, ships that can get up into the Chesapeake, but can't put in at a port."

Max nodded. "A big operation. All right, so we know where the runners are going, but how does the Devil's Elbow light fit into all this?"

"Just north of Crisfield, you have three major rivers, the Manokin, the Wicomico, and the Nanticoke. They each are roadways to and from the interior of the lower Eastern Shore. The Nanticoke goes all the way to Salisbury, so these rivers can carry the output of hundreds of stills out to the customers. But there's a string of islands to get past first, so to get to and from the bay, you have to go through Hooper Strait or Kedges Strait. The Devil's Elbow light is on the bay side of Kedges strait, south of the Devil's Elbow Bar, a shallow area sticking out from South Marsh Island." As he was talking, Brian Murphy was drawing a diagram on a napkin with a pencil stub.

"Now if that light keeper was to look for runners, he'd have a hard time seeing any until they were less than a mile from him."

"Because they run at night and without lights," said Max.

"Right. Plus a light keeper has the light constantly rotating over his head messing up his night vision. And by the time a runner is within a mile or so of the light, he's out in the broad part of the bay if he's heading west, so he can lose anyone real easy. If he's heading east, he's only a few miles from Crisfield and a hundred little coves he can duck into before anybody got close."

"So you're saying that an observer in the lighthouse wouldn't be that much help to the police or the Coast Guard?"

"He might be of some help spotting traffic during the day, but that's when all the workboats are out, so there is no way of telling who might be a runner without a stop and search, so observations from the light house wouldn't be much use. Besides, during the day the only runners are workboats with false decks and cubbyholes. A boat like that can only carry maybe 30 gallons or so. The big loads move at night when they can cram the hold and even the decks with the goods. A runner needs concealment during the day and evasion at night. No, Mr. Hurlock, the theory that rum runners wanted to silence Coleman is a lot of bunk. He couldn't be a problem, not enough to commit murder over, anyway."

"I see what you mean," said Max. "Brian could you check with your, er, associates and see if any of them were in Kedges Strait that night?"

"Max, I told you my boys wouldn't have any reason to kill Jack Coleman."

"I understand," Max assured him, "but whoever dropped in at the light that night had to have gotten there by boat. If one of your boys saw that boat and could describe it..."

Brian Murphy nodded and stood up to leave. "I'll ask around. Thanks for breakfast."

Max's next stop was Paisley's Tavern, now since Prohibition known as the Paisley Club, a speakeasy that also served food. The Paisley Club was housed in a wood building that looked as if it hadn't seen a coat of paint since Theodore Roosevelt was president, if then. Max walked up and encountered a locked door. An eye appeared at a peephole and a female voice told Max the club didn't open until six.

"I'm looking for Nell Paisley. I'm Max Hurlock."

There was a pause, then the sound of a latch opening. Inside the club was gloomy and quiet and Max found himself face to face with Nell Paisley. With no wind to toss her hair and no exasperation in her expression, she looked younger and more in control than she had at the lighthouse.

"You were out at the light with Fred Bentley and those watermen, weren't you?"

"That's right. I'm trying to find out what happened to Jack Coleman and I sure could use your help."

"You never found any diary?"

"No, and I went over the place thoroughly."

"I don't know what I could tell you that would help. I just run a club here."

Max smiled. "A lot of speakeasies call themselves clubs nowadays, don't they?"

"What? Who told you this place was a speakeasy?"

"Look around. A club that doesn't open until six with a peephole to check people who want to come in; rows of folding shelves to dispose of bottles in a hurry; stacks of teacups so everything looks innocent; several conspicuous sinks to quickly dispose of the evidence; and what appears to be two extra doors for a quick exit out the back in case of a raid. If it isn't a speakeasy, you've wasted a lot of money."

"All right, Mr. Hurlock. What do you want?"

"Just some information. What did Jack Coleman do to get thrown out a few weeks ago?"

"You won't tell my husband?"

"Not unless the case depends on it, but I suspect it doesn't."

Nell Paisley sat in a wooden chair at one of the tables. She seemed equal parts weary and exasperated. "Jack was a strange man. He was always complaining about how lonely it was out there, and how he was watching everybody's comings and goings; said he knew who went where and when they went there. Everyone thought it was just talk. The more he drank the more he talked. Then one night, he was outside looking at the moon and I came out to dump some trash. He grabbed my arm and started saying how he wanted me to stop by the lighthouse for a visit. I just laughed it off and forgot about it. Then a few weeks later, he was back and pulling the same old bushwa. I told him I wasn't interested and to stop it before Tom found out and gave him a thumping. This went on for weeks and I was desperate that Tom not find out. Tom's very jealous and I didn't know what he'd do if he thought Jack was pursuing me."

"I assume he never did find out?"

"If he did, he kept quiet about it. Well, this went on for two months and finally I told Jack that if he ever showed his face at the club again, I'd tell Tom. Well, that made Jack nasty. He said he was keeping a diary of all the drinks he'd had at the club and all the liquor violations he'd seen. He said there were some things about me in that diary, too, things other people would be very interested in. He walked away that night, but said he'd be back and if I didn't let him in, he'd send the diary to the police and the newspapers."

"So that's why you wanted the diary?"

"Yes, if there even is a diary. It could have been the gin talking."

"So did he come back?"

"Just once, about a week before he was killed in fact."

"And did you tell him he couldn't come in?"

Nell shook her head. "I didn't have to. Tom spotted him before he ever got to the door and they had a terrible cursing match. I think a customer must have tipped Tom off that Jack Coleman was making advances towards me, or maybe Tom had seen us and not let on. Anyway, Tom said he knew Jack was fooling around with me and that he'd pay for it. Then Tom took a swing at him and Jack Coleman backed off. That seemed to make Tom even madder and he said he was going to come out to that lighthouse and settle the score once and for all."

"I see."

"I know what you're thinking, Mr. Hurlock, but I'm sure Tom didn't mean it. He liked to bluster. Tom's a big man and he usually gets his way with just a threat. He just wanted to scare Jack away."

"Well..."

"Who the hell are you?" came a gruff voice. Max turned around and saw a big stocky man standing behind him and looking very unfriendly.

"Ah; you must be Mr. Paisley. Your wife was just telling me about what a fine establishment you have here."

"Humph. So you just stopped by to compliment the food, eh?"

"Not exactly. I'm Max Hurlock and I'm talking to everyone I can to see if anyone knows anything about the death of that lighthouse keeper out at the Devil's Elbow."

"And you think Nell knows about it, do you?"

"Well, you never know who might have heard something. Did Jack Coleman come in the club often?"

"Yeah," Tom Paisley snarled, "once too often."

"What do you mean?" Max asked.

Tom Paisley took a step closer. "I mean it's time for you to be on your way and to ask your damned questions somewhere else."

Gaston Means was waiting for Max on the porch of the Commercial Hotel and greeted him warmly.

"Ah, Mr. Hurlock. It's good to see you again."

"Hello, Mr. Means. Anything to report?"

Means leaned forward in his chair and spoke to Max in a conspiratorial fashion.

"I am pleased to report that our Mr. Smith appeared last night as promised. He has some wonderful news."

"Yes?"

"It seems that the bootlegger syndicate has been remiss in paying their rent, and the landlord is unhappy about it. Well, the landlord has duplicate keys to both the office and the locked closet and he has agreed to allow Mr. Smith to use them to obtain the box with the incriminating documents."

"Great. When will he bring them?"

Means's smile faded. "He can have then in a day or two, but there is a difficulty. It seems the landlord wishes to be paid for his trouble, and to make up the rent he's owed. He is asking for the money up front."

Max frowned. "I see. How much?"

"Five thousand dollars."

"That's a lot of rent."

"And for his trouble."

"Well, I'm sure the federal government can certainly scrape together the money if it means cracking the case," Max suggested.

Means frowned as if in pain. "If only it were that simple, but the Bureau of Investigation has a strict policy of not paying anonymous sources for information."

"I see."

"So I'm afraid that leaves me in a bit of a quandary," Means sighed. "Without the funds to pay this man, I have no evidence that would point to anyone but your friends as the killers of Jack Coleman."

Max said nothing. There was an awkward silence as Means shook his head slowly. Max still did not speak.

"Of course," said Means slowly, "if the necessary money were to come from some other source, I doubt that Mr. Smith would care. Perhaps you could prevail upon your friends to put up the money in their own defense. I'm sure a defense attorney in a trial would cost as much."

Max stood up and put on his hat.

"I see. I'll have to get back to you."

Max returned to the Hotel Continental and put through a call to Allison back in St Michaels.

"So how did you and the dear departed get along?" Max asked.

"Like chalk and cheese. Max, that was the spookiest thing I've ever witnessed. I kept telling myself that everything was a trick of some kind, but now I don't know what to think. If you couple that with Madame DeSousa's remarks about me when we first met, I'm beginning to wonder if this spirit stuff is real after all."

"Madame DeSousa or her assistant couldn't have been doing all this in the dark?"

"Max, everyone was holding hands, and I had my foot on one of her feet, so she couldn't have even used that."

"Spooky."

Allison sighed "Anyway, how are you doing with the light house keeper case? Any developments?"

"Oh yes. A federal agent is trying to extort money from me."

"What? Are you serious?"

Max explained his meetings with Gaston Means.

"Are you sure he isn't on the up and up?" Allison asked. "Sometimes you take a dislike to someone for no apparent reason."

"The reasons are always apparent to me," Max retorted. "The man seemed oily from the first. Sergeant Bentley called him a grifter in a ten dollar suit. Means's story is too pat and too lacking in details. I talked to people on the waterfront and he hadn't interviewed any of them. Besides, I know he's lying about Mr. Smith coming to see him last night."

"And how do you know that?"

"Because I sat in the lobby of his hotel until almost eleven last night. I was seated where I could see the door of Means's room, but he couldn't see me. He went out to the Lyric theater across the street until after ten. Then he returned and went straight to his room. He had no visitors."

"A stake out to check a story? Watch it Max. You're starting to act like a detective."

"Perish the thought. Anyway, I'm going to be back home late this afternoon, if Gypsy holds out. I'm going to materialize right in your arms, and we're going to do more than just hold hands."

"Now that's the spirit!"

John Reisinger

Chapter 12

Squeeze play

Bentley gave Max a lift back to the farm where he had stowed Gypsy. On the way, Max told him about his meeting with Gaston Means.

"So Means is trying to squeeze you, eh? I can't say I'm surprised. He seemed to be pretty casual about how he was investigating because he wasn't really investigating at all, just lining up a few suspects to milk them for money. Did you tell Means you were on to him?"

Max shook his head. "No. I didn't see any gain from telling him. I thought I'd play along for a while and see what happens."

"I'll keep an eye on him as best I can in Crisfield, and I'll keep asking people about Jack Coleman."

"Thanks, Fred. Maybe you could help in another way."

"What's that?"

"I suppose you know most of the doctors around here?"

"I reckon that's a fact."

"Maybe you could ask around and see if any of them recently patched up someone with knife wounds."

Bentley smiled. "I've been doing that already. Been through about half of them without much luck, but I'll let you know if anything turns up."

"Thanks. One more thing; what do you know about the Paisleys?"

"Which one?"

"Let's start with Nell. Could she be lying about throwing Coleman out of the Paisley Club? You know; maybe covering up a real affair?"

"Well, now that you mention it, there have been rumors. Jack Coleman was known as a dab hand with the ladies, and Nell doesn't always get along well with her husband Tom. Nell and Billy Thebold got real friendly a year ago and Tom found out and was ready to put the kibosh on both of them. I got a call from the Paisley Club one night and when I got there I found Billy Thebold knocked out on the floor and Tom pounding on the bathroom door where Nell had locked herself in. It took me and two other men to subdue old Tom."

"So Nell seeing another man is possible?"

"I'd say so. Nell gets restless now and again, I suppose; needs a change of scene, so to speak. They have spats about it, but always seem to get back together."

"And if she really was seeing Jack Coleman, I imagine she would go to great lengths to keep Tom in the dark, knowing his violent tendencies."

"Now you're on the trolley, Max. That there is a woman with a guilty secret. If she was carrying on with Jack Coleman, the less Tom knew the better."

"How about her story that Tom threatened to come to the lighthouse and settle the score?"

"That sounds like Tom, and it would certainly explain why J.D. and No Whiskey found Jack Coleman so spooked when they dropped in on him."

"Yes, it would," said Max, "but then why would he let in a visitor and drink coffee with him just a few hours later?"

Bentley shook his head as if to clear it. "Well, I can't say."

"What if Nell wanted to end the affair and Coleman threatened to tell the world?" asked Max. "Maybe Coleman had a tell-all diary, or claimed he did. Could she have killed Coleman to get the diary? Tom was angry and suspicious, but maybe he never knew all the sordid details. Could Nell have dropped in on Jack Coleman and killed him to keep Tom from finding out the extent of the affair? That would certainly explain why Coleman let his killer in and served coffee."

"Well, maybe," said Bentley thoughtfully. "'Course, there's another possibility."

"Oh. And what's that?"

"Maybe Tom *did* find out and saved her the trouble."

Allison was waiting as Max rolled Gypsy to a halt by the barn.

"Am I glad to see you," she cooed. "If I had to face another night alone with the sounds of nature around here, I'd have to check into a hotel."

"It's nice to be appreciated. Do you still feel confused about the séance?"

"I slept with the light on last night. Does that answer your question? Come next Halloween, I'm hiding under the bed. And if any crockery moves in the house it had better have a hand on it. How about you? Are there any new developments at Crisfield?

Max recounted his conversations with Nell and Tom Paisley.

"That sounds like a good situation to stay out of; bootleggers, jealous husbands, rumrunners, and a sleazy federal agent. I'd say it's time to wash your hands of the whole sordid affair."

"I'm afraid I can't. I'll have to tell J.D. and No Whiskey what happened."

"Well, of course, but what of it? You promised to ask around and you did. They can't expect more than that."

"I thought that would be the end of it, but it isn't. Now I'm hooked. I can't quit until I find out who killed the light keeper."

"Can't quit? But why?"

"Don't you see? Means is trying to blackmail J.D. and No Whiskey through me. If he doesn't get the money, he'll file charges on them. The only way I can protect them is by solving the case before he does that."

"Pooh. I think that Mr. Means is just a lot of wind."

"So's a hurricane."

"But surely he doesn't have any real evidence."

"No, but he has enough to give them months of worry, uncertainty, and expense. That's what he's counting on to shake the money loose."

"That snake! I hope you gave him a piece of your mind."

"No, I didn't. I'll let him think I'm fooled and maybe he'll drop his guard long enough for me to nail him somehow."

"So what happens if you do give him the money? Wouldn't he have to deliver?"

"No. Then there'd be some new difficulty that just arose. He'd claim someone else was demanding money; maybe a member of the bootlegging syndicate or a passerby that saw Smith rifling the closet. No, Means would invent new stories to string it out until he squeezed every penny, then claim Smith had disappeared and taken the money with him."

"Whew," said Allison. "I used to think you had a suspicious mind, but apparently you're just being realistic."

That evening, Max had an animated conversation on the telephone while Allison worked on some notes on the porch. Presently he appeared beside her.

"I just talked to J.D., since No Whiskey doesn't have a phone. They're both scared of being charged with murder in a federal court. They want to raise the money to pay Means."

"They're going to pay that rat? Didn't you tell them it was a shell game?"

"They're clutching at straws at this point. J.D. is talking about getting a loan by putting up his boat and his house as collateral."

"Oh, no. That boat's how he earns a living."

"So now I have to solve the case to pull the rug out from under Means and save J.D. and Calvin's homes and livelihoods. Oh, my aching back."

Allison stood up and kissed Max on the cheek.

"Once more into the soup, dear friends…"

Max put his arm around her. "I'm sorry, Allison. I didn't want to get involved in this mess, but now I have to. J.D. and No Whiskey could be ruined if I don't."

She smiled. "My hero; riding to the rescue of those in need. All you need is a white horse."

"I'm afraid I'll need a lot more than that before this is over."

"What will you do next?"

"I'm thinking of checking with the Coast Guard office in Baltimore and seeing if they have any vessel reports from that night, or maybe some information about boats they've stopped. Maybe something will match up. I'll check with the Lighthouse Service as well, in case Coleman filed any reports that could be revealing."

Allison didn't answer right away, but picked up a newspaper and started thumbing through it.

"Can you wait until next Tuesday?"

"I suppose so. Why?"

"Well, my information on Madame DeSousa mentioned that she started out working with a woman named Irene Sterling in Baltimore. Sterling is now a big name medium in that town. I thought if I went to one of her séances, I could see if they use the same tricks and maybe I could figure it out."

"Makes sense…"

"And the very next night, Houdini is appearing at the Hippodrome. We could go to see him while we're in town. He puts on a great show and he usually exposes some medium tricks."

"Isn't he on some kind of a mission to expose mediums?"

"That's right, so I'd get oodles of great material for my article, and we'd see a wonderful show besides."

"All right. We go Tuesday. That will give me time to check with Duffy Merkle."

"Ah, the industrious Mr. Merkle; purveyor of fine spirits to a grateful and thirsty public, and another of your very interesting friends. Be careful you don't get any moonshine splashed on your new trousers. It might eat a hole in them."

The road to Duffy Merkle's place was easy to miss, and appeared to be not so much a driveway as a twisted and muddy path through vine encrusted woods. Low branches slapped the sides of Max's Model T as it lurched along.

"For crying out loud Duffy. How do you get your product out of here?"

Suddenly, the path became a straight, well maintained drive, and Max realized the overgrown entrance was designed to discourage casual visitors.

In a few minutes, he came to a small, neat white house next to several barns and animal pens. A gate across the road stopped him well short of the house.

"Hold it right there," came a voice. "You're trespassing on private property. Now you just turn that flivver around and get out."

In the doorway of the nearest barn stood a stocky, bearded man with a shotgun.

"I'm looking for Duffy Merkle," Max shouted. The man lowered the shotgun barrel and shaded his eyes as he looked in Max's direction.

"Hey, Max. Is that you? Well why didn't you say so? Come on in."

Duffy opened the gate and Max pulled up in front of the house.

"What brings you out here, Max? Do you want to see my operation?"

"I want some information on rum running, and I figure you're an expert."

"Sure thing. Like what?"

"Well, I know there are dozens of runners zipping in and out of rivers and coves on the Eastern Shore, but who are they and where do they hole up during the day?"

Duffy laughed. "Well, shoot. That ain't no mystery. They're mostly watermen during the day and what you might call businessmen at night. Here, I'll show you."

Duffy led Max into the biggest barn. It looked normal inside, but contained a still hidden behind some stalls and hay.

"This here's the mash cooker," he said, indicating a large tank with a small fire under it. "We put cornmeal in there along with some sugar and yeast, and let it ferment awhile so's the alcohol forms."

Max smelled the pungent mix and coughed slightly.

"Now water boils at 212 degrees, but alcohol boils at 173, so you keep it cookin' around 190, hot enough to boil off the alcohol but leave the water behind along with the mash. So now you got alcohol steam and you run it through this curly copper tube here so the alcohol steam cools down and the alcohol condenses like the water of the side of a lemonade pitcher in the summertime. You collect the alcohol, bottle it up, and there you are."

"Ingenious," said Max. "Somehow, my college chemistry courses never got into such practical matters. Anyway, what about distribution and delivery?"

"That depends on where the customer is located. If the customer is local and inland, I ship it out in trucks or in runner cars with secret compartments. For customers on the Western Shore, I have a runner pick it up at my dock back here on the creek."

"That's where Brian Murphy comes in, I suppose."

"Sure, sometimes. It all depends."

"On what?"

"I have my own customers and my own arrangements, had most of 'em for years, but with

Brian, I get to supply a wider distribution you might say. I get to be part of a pool of moonshiners. He arranges for transportation, payment, everything. As far as I'm concerned, it's easy money. Plus, it's safer."

"How come?"

"Well, let's say I'm shipping lots of product to the Western Shore by boats from my pier and the Prohibition police get wind of it and start watchin' the creek. I'd have to shut down until it blows over. But if I tell Brian Murphy, he'll arrange for it to be trucked to another creek and another runner until the heat is off."

"And for that service, you pay him a percentage?"

"It's worth every penny, Max."

"Have you ever heard a runner complain about somebody in a lighthouse reporting on them to the Coast Guard?"

"No. Never. Far as I can see, it's just like Brian told you. Whatever that light keeper was doing, it wasn't reporting runners to the Coast Guard."

Max tried another tack. "Duffy, do you know many people in Crisfield?"

"Quite a few. I got a cousin, P.J. who lives there."

"How about Nell Paisley?"

Duffy was silent a moment, looking down at the ground. "Come on in the house and we can talk about it."

Duffy Merkle's house was surprisingly neat and tidy, a tribute more to Mrs. Merkle than Duffy. She was not at home, so there was only Duffy's old black Labrador retriever for company.

"This here's old Midnight. We've done a lot of duck gunnin' together. He's gettin' old now, but then again, I guess I am too."

Max scratched Midnight behind the ear and they sat in two mismatched armchairs. Duffy's beard bristled and his belly strained his overalls as he sat down.

"Nell Paisley. The Paisleys are a funny pair," Duffy began. "They came to Crisfield about ten years ago. Tom was a butcher someplace, least that's what the story is, and Nell ran some kind of restaurant. Anyway, the wonder is how the two of them ever thought getting hitched was a good idea. They're always squabblin' about something. Tom has a bad temper and Nell has a stubborn streak. What's worse, Tom has a rovin' eye and has been chasin' half the women in Crisfield at one time of another."

"I suppose Nell wasn't too happy about that," said Max.

"Not much, but the rumor is that she's been known to have a fling or two herself. Anyway, a year ago it was Billy Thebold from over Deal Island. Billy was just a kid really, but Nell is a good looking woman and Billy sort of lost his head over her. He was just back from some college on the Western Shore and somehow met up with Nell. He'd come to the club and order drinks just to talk to her. I can't say if it ever went any farther than that, but Billy was smitten, no doubt about it."

"Until Tom found out?" asked Max.

"Until Tom found out. Then all hell busted loose. Now, I wasn't there, mind you, so this is all second hand, but I understand Tom confronted Billy and there was a very short fight that ended with Billy getting knocked out on the club floor. When Billy came to, he swore he'd get even. Nobody in Crisfield's seen Billy much since then. Maybe he just gave up on Nell."

"Maybe."

Or maybe he's just been biding his time, Max thought.

"What about Jack Coleman, the lighthouse keeper?" Max asked.

"I heard tell different things about that. Some say Nell was carryin' on with him somethin' fierce. Some even say she'd visit him at the lighthouse when she'd told Tom she was going to see her mother in Salisbury. Others say it was all a show to get under Tom's skin to get back at him for what he done to Billy."

"What ever happened to Billy?"

Duffy scratched his beard thoughtfully.

"Hard to say. He never went back to the club, and got a job up in Salisbury they say. Folk that know him say he's still got a hatred for Tom Paisley and still wants his revenge, but he's lyin' low. Maybe he's just too busy."

"Yeah, maybe," said Max, but he did not sound convinced.

John Reisinger

Chapter 13

Restless spirits

Allison already had her bags packed for their trip to Baltimore next Tuesday. Now she sat down at the old Olivetti typewriter and began her article.

The Lure of Spiritualism
By Allison Hurlock

Can we communicate with the dead? It would seem to be a ridiculous question, but many people believe the answer is yes. A curiosity about the afterlife has been around for centuries, and today's spiritualism dates back to the last century, but the crushing death tolls of the Great War and the Spanish flu epidemic that followed generated vast numbers of people grieving for loved ones who died suddenly at a young age. This powerful yearning for some contact with those so cruelly taken has been a powerful push to a revival of spiritualism.

Today, few towns lack a resident spiritualist who gives readings and conducts séances to communicate with the dead. Are these people real, or are they just charlatans out to bilk the gullible?

She looked at what she had typed.
"All right, Allison," she said out loud. "You asked the obvious question. Now how are you going to answer it?"
At a recent séance with a well-known medium in a small town in Maryland, trumpets danced in the air, a light dimmed and brightened, and a table rose and rocked back and forth, all while the medium and the guests were holding hands. A translucent ball of Ectoplasm even made an appearance, hanging eerily over everyone's head. If it was all a trick it was a pretty good one.

"You know, sooner or later, I'm going to have to actually express a conclusion one way or another, but at the moment, I don't know what to think."
She pushed back from the table and stretched. Then she placed a phone call to Isis Dalrymple, the town librarian.
"Hey Isis. Thanks again for that dirt you dug up on Madame DeSousa. Are you going in to town today? Max has the flivver and I don't feel like walking all the way to the center of St Michaels."
"I was just about to depart for the metropolis *tout suite* to pick up some sustenance at the local emporium. Would you like to share my motorized conveyance, perchance?"
"I would be honored to share your chariot," said Allison, getting into the spirit of the thing. Soon they

were rattling down the road on their way to the center of town.

"Isis, what do you think of spiritualism?" Allison asked casually.

Isis, a short round woman with black unruly hair stuffed into a gray hat looked interested. She adjusted her glasses before replying, a sure sign she was about to give an opinion at great length.

"Communicating with the spirit world has been a subject of interest forever. At the moment, spiritualism is enjoying a bit of a revival, but it's only the latest round of science against superstition."

"But many people seem to be convinced of it," Allison reminded her, "even Arthur Conan Doyle."

"Conan Doyle should reread about ratiocination as laid out in some of his marvelous Sherlock Holmes stories. Holmes would never come to that conclusion based on such flimsy evidence. However, 'The sleep of reason brings forth monsters' as Goya so aptly put it, or painted it, to be more precise. I suppose reason doesn't really enter the picture. It's more a will to believe, as William James once said."

"I see," said Allison, although she wasn't sure she saw at all.

Isis Dalrymple dropped Allison off at the cannery at Navy Point in St Michaels just as the oyster shuckers were getting off for the day. Since it was Friday, they were paid just after noon and the cannery closed down for the rest of the day. Allison waited as the lines of women, many with their children filed out. The rubber boots, aprons and gloves had been stowed in lockers and the scene looked normal, except for the fishy odor that hung over everything. Finally, she saw Mabel Johnson.

"Hello, Allison. What brings you to the cannery?"

"I wanted to talk with you. Come on. I'll buy you lunch."

St Michaels was not a town known for its restaurants, so they stopped at the drug store on the road that passed through town. When they had settled at the counter and ordered sandwiches and Cliquot Club ginger ales, the extent of the menu, Allison spoke.

"Mabel, I've been researching an article on spiritualism and I wanted to ask you about Madame DeSousa."

Mabel's face, usually a gray mask of worry, lit up with a dreamy far-away look.

"Madame DeSousa is a saint. Thanks to her spiritual powers, I can be in contact with Harold, even though he's passed over. Knowing I can have Harold's presence and advice has gotten me through many a night, I can tell you."

"How often do you go to her?"

"Oh, off and on. I go when I need to talk to Harold, maybe once every month or two."

"But how can you be sure that it's really Harold? Couldn't Madame DeSousa be, well, faking it?"

Their sandwiches were plunked down on the green countertop, and Mabel was quiet for a while as she munched and considered the question.

"Allison, I know you write articles and you're real smart and all, so you have to question everything and look for flaws…"

Allison started to object, but thought better of it.

"…Well, I don't know about all that stuff. I never finished high school and I never been any farther than Ocean City. I just know this." She reached in her pocket, pulled out her oyster shucking knife and placed it on the counter. The wooden handle was over twice as long as the short sturdy blade.

"This belonged to Harold. Now that he's gone, it's all I have to depend on. This is all I have to make a living. Oyster after oyster, bushel after bushel, and day after day, this is my life. My hands and Harold's knife are all I got in this world. But Madame DeSousa gives me something more. She gives me a feeling of security; a feeling of hope. She makes me think that in some small way, Harold is still up there looking out for me. He gave me this knife and now he's still giving me his guidance. You can't put a price on that."

Allison nodded and put her hand on Mabel's shoulder. "Mabel, I don't think I've ever written anything as eloquent as what you just said. Thank you."

There was another silence. Allison looked at the knife and thought of all the weary hours of oyster shucking it had seen in Mabel's hands. The wooden handle was worn and stained from hard use, and the blade was shiny for the same reason. Then Allison noticed something.

"Mabel, did you say Harold left this knife?"

"That's right. He did some shucking one winter a couple of years ago when he hurt his leg."

"Do you know where Harold got it?"

"I think he got it from some fella over in Cambridge who makes knives. Has a forge and everything."

"Do you know the man's name?"

"His name? Oh, let's see. I really don't know. I never met him, but Harold raved about his work. Said he had some special way of workin' the steel so it wouldn't snap as easily. I'm not sure Harold ever mentioned a name; leastwise, I can't remember one. Why? What does it have to do with spiritualism?"

"Oh, nothing, really," said Allison. "Just curious. Did you notice the wavy lines in the blade?"

Mabel picked up the knife. She looked at the blade and shrugged. "Never thought about it. All I know is this knife gets the job done. Besides, I like having something of Harold's with me all day. It gives me a comfort somehow, like some small part of Harold is still here. Does that sound strange?"

"No," said Allison, "it doesn't sound strange at all."

Isis Dalrymple picked Allison up an hour later to return home. Since Isis was an authority on almost everything, Allison asked her if she had any idea why knives would have faint lines on the blade.

"Metallurgy," said Isis. "That's a folded steel blade you're talking about."

"Folded? You mean like a jackknife?"

"No, no. The steel is heated and hammered on an anvil. The steel is bent in half, like folding a piece of paper, and then heated and bent again. The steel gets layers in it from the times it was folded over and reflattened. That drives out impurities and allows making blades out of two kinds of metal for strength and flexibility. The Japanese make swords that way, so do the Hindus."

"And that folding makes the lines?"

"Right. I think the hot steel gets quenched in some kind of acid bath after it's finished folding and that makes the lines. It's a slow and expensive way to work steel, but it makes the blade extra tough."

"Amazing. Isis, is there anything you don't know?"

Isis looked thoughtful. "I don't know."

Max stopped by J.D. Pratt's place on his way back from seeing Duffy Merkle and found him just returning with Casper Nowitsky from a day of oyster tonging. As they tied the Karen Rebecca to the rickety dock, Max looked at his pocket watch.

"You boys are back early."

"We didn't go to the cannery," said J.D. "There was a buy boat out there paying cash money and we sold the catch to him. We do that most days. It saves time so's we can catch more or knock off early."

"Very smart."

J.D. and Casper stepped onto the dock. "So, how are you doing, Max? Have you found out anything about who killed Jack Coleman?"

"I found out there are several people who might have wanted him dead for one reason or another, but nothing conclusive so far. Are you still figuring on paying Means?"

"What choice do we have, Max?" said Casper. "He represents the federal government. You can't fight them. If they come after us, they'll wear us down to a nub."

"He wants the money," said Max. "He doesn't have a case and he knows it. All he has is the information that you were there hours before the body was found, including about eight hours of darkness when anyone else could have come calling. I don't care if he does represent the federal government. If they go to court and that's all the evidence they have, they'll be thrown out in a minute."

"Maybe so," said Casper, "but in the meantime, we'll be in the slammer if we can't raise bail, and we can't afford to be away from the water so long. The way we see it, we have to raise money either way."

Max sat on a box on the side of the pier and sighed.

"Well, I know how things should be, but I can't guarantee how they will be," he said. "You boys have to do what you think is best. All I can say is I'll try to get to the bottom of it. Just promise me you'll tell me before you hand any money over to Gaston Means."

"All right, Max. We'll surely do that."

Max nodded. "Fair enough. Now, you boys get around and you know every boat around here pretty much, so what do you hear from the other watermen? Has anyone heard any rumors or scuttlebutt about the case?"

J.D. exhaled heavily. "That's a tall order, Max. See, ever since Prohibition, we been seein' a lot of new faces around here. People come from Virginia and the Western Shore to set up brewin' operations where the distribution is good and the enforcement is bad. I heard tell a couple of 'em worked at the big breweries back when they were legal. Some of 'em turn out a mighty good product, so I'm told. Anyway, every night there's boats comin' and goin' every which way around here. We don't know who they all are."

"How about Brian Murphy?"

Casper chimed in. "I met him back before Prohibition. He was scraping by with hand tongin'. Seemed like a smart fella; always had some kind of scheme. I figured he'd go places."

"How about Billy Thebold?"

J.D. answered. "I met him down south of Crisfield a couple of years ago. He was working on a skipjack drudgin' arsters around Pocomoke Sound and we were hove to, waitin' on the same buy boat and got to talking. He was just out of some college and was working to get some money to get started up in Salisbury."

"Started doing what?"

"He didn't say, but one thing I could tell for sure; that was one determined fella. Once he got an idea in his head, weren't nothin' that could stop him."

Max raised his eyebrows slightly.

"Even if that idea was revenge?"

Casper nodded. "I'd say *especially* if that idea was revenge."

That night Max and Allison had fried Rockfish for dinner, along with some asparagus from the garden and some bread Allison had picked up in town.

"How's the fish, Max?" she asked anxiously. "It's not burned too badly, is it?"

"Not at all," said Max, bravely. "After all, a little charcoal helps the digestion."

"I still haven't quite gotten the hang of this cooking thing," said Allison, poking a piece of fish with her fork, "but I think I'm getting better."

"Yes, there's definite improvement. Soon you'll be opening our own restaurant. You can call it Allison Hurlock's Dinner Bucket: Food like mother used to make."

"If she was cooking blindfolded, you mean."

"Speaking of things to chew on," said Max, "I talked to J.D. and Casper today. They're trying to take out loans to pay off Gaston Means."

"That sounds like a really bad investment. You'd better hurry and solve the case before they do it."

"Sure; what's a little more pressure?"

"Oh, I talked to Mabel Johnson again. She swears by Madame DeSousa."

"That's not really surprising. I'm sure she gets some comfort from the arrangement. The problem is; can she afford it?"

"We didn't discuss that part, but I intend to take it up with Madame DeSousa. Anyway, a curious thing happened. Mabel showed me the shucking knife Harold had left her and it had the kind of faint lines in the blade that you talked about when you described the knife that was at the lighthouse. I asked Isis about it afterwards and she said the lines are from a blacksmith technique of folding the steel to make the blade stronger."

"Hmmm. Interesting."

"I don't really think Mabel noticed the lines before, but she did say Harold got the knife from some man in Cambridge who forges the things at home. She couldn't remember his name, though."

"Or if he's still alive and still around," said Max. "Even so, it's a possible clue. Maybe he kept a ledger of his customers, that is, assuming that's where the knife came from."

"Whew!" said Allison. "If a horse was that much of a long shot at Pimlico, nobody would bet on him."

The next morning, Max took the Model T and headed south to Cambridge, another seafood and tomato cannery town on the Choptank River. He took the ferry across the Choptank and drove to the Cambridge Police station by the courthouse. It didn't take long to find someone who knew about the Cambridge man who made knives at his home forge. The man was Pat Dolan and he lived just outside of town. Max was there in a few minutes.

The Dolan place had once been a farm, but was overgrown now. Although well kept, the house appeared empty, at least at the moment. As Max stood by the front door, he heard a metallic clanging sound and followed it around the back.

There was an old barn behind the house and the metallic clanging sound seemed to come from there. Max looked in the door of the barn and thought he was in Dante's Inferno. A huge man was silhouetted by the glowing coals of a forge as he pounded a piece of red hot metal on an anvil, throwing sparks with every strike. He turned around and saw Max.

"Be with ya in a second."

A few more ringing metallic poundings and he placed the metal back in the coals.

"Good Morning. I'm Max Hurlock and I'm looking for Pat Dolan."

The man wiped the sweat off his forehead with his sleeve.

"That's me. You want a knife?"

"Actually, I'm looking for information about a knife with a folded steel blade."

"Right. I make those. I'm retired from the railroad, you see. I was the foreman of the repair shop, so I learned something about metals and heating steel. I've been making farm tools and knives for the past five years. I'm the only one making Damascus blades around here as far as I know."

"Do you have samples handy?"

"Right over there." Dolan pointed to a board with several knives of different sizes stuck in it. Max stopped when he came to the third one; it was the knife they had found in the lighthouse, right down to the lines in the blade.

"How about this one? Do you sell many of these?"

"Oh, maybe twenty or thirty a year. They're popular with hunters and watermen because the blades can take a lot of abuse and still keep an edge."

Max picked up the knife. "This has a good feel to it. The craftsmanship is superb. How much is it?"

"Seven dollars for the standard one, but I can make the blade a custom size if you'd like. I can put on an ivory handle if you'd prefer, but that runs up the cost."

"Mr. Dolan, do you keep a record of your sales and who bought from you?"

Dolan's smile faded and he looked at Max with suspicion. "Sure; *confidential* records."

"I understand your concern with your customers' privacy, Mr. Dolan, but a knife like this was found at the scene of the murder of the lighthouse keeper down near Crisfield. If the police come around here, they could get a court order and take all your records. I'm not with the police. I'm a private investigator. I can't do that and I wouldn't want to. All I need are a few names. Then maybe the crime would get solved and no one would have to grab your records."

"Any name you're looking for in particular?"

"Several names," said Max. "I'm just not sure which one at this point."

Dolan looked at Max a moment, as if sizing him up.

"Well, I'll tell you what. You give me a list of the names you're looking for and I'll look through my records when I get a chance. If I find any matches, I'll call you up on the telephone."

"I really could use the information now, Mr. Dolan."

"And I really could use some solitude," Dolan snapped. "I said I'd look through my records and I will. If that's not fast enough, maybe the police can be faster."

Max realized a huge man who pounded red hot metal all day could probably not be pushed easily. He took out a sheet of paper and began to write names.

"All right, Mr. Dolan. Here are the names and here is the number of the St Michaels operator. Just ask her to connect you with Max Hurlock, but please be as quick as you can. I'm afraid that without this information the authorities are going to accuse a couple of my watermen friends who had nothing to do with it."

Dolan took the paper and stuffed it in his pocket without looking at it and returned to his work pounding a piece of red hot steel.

John Reisinger

Chapter 14

Crisfield again

The telephone was ringing in the hall early the next morning. Allison was the first to wake up enough to notice.

"Any time that thing rings this early, it has to be bad news. Do you want to get it, Max?"

"All right," Max groaned. "What's a little more bad news at this point?"

Max stumbled towards the telephone while Allison put on her blue Chenille robe and followed him yawning.

"All right, J.D. When do you expect to get there? ...Well wait for me, O.K.?"

He placed the black earpiece back into its cradle.

"J.D. and Casper are going to Crisfield to talk to Means about a payment schedule. I told them I'd meet them there. Maybe I can keep this from getting out of hand."

"A little late for that," said Allison, "but at least you can be a restraining influence. Well, get dressed and I'll make some coffee. I assume you're taking Gypsy?"

"That's right."

"I'll go with you."

"That's fine, but why?"

"Maybe I could talk to some of the local women and get their thoughts on the Nell Paisley- Tom Paisley- Billy Thebold- Jack Coleman situation. They'd be more candid with me than with you."

"Don't bet on it," said Max. "You're still an outsider, but if you want to come along, fine."

Fred Bentley picked Max and Allison up after a phone call. He was especially glad to see Allison, and reluctant to drop her off in town before proceeding to the dock area.

"Now you just call if you need anything," he assured her.

Allison smiled sweetly. "I sure will, Sergeant. Thank you so much."

"All right, Max," he said, still smiling, "where are you supposed to meet J.D. and Casper?"

"The steamboat pier, I think. I'll recognize their boat when they come in. I guess I've got a few minutes. Have there been any developments in the last couple of days?"

"There was a reporter named Hal Marks from the Evening Sun down here asking around yesterday. Means has been nosing around a bit, but not with any real purpose as far as I can tell. The Coast Guard has been stopping by more than usual and the runners have been pretty quiet. I heard tell of a big shipment due to go out of here is a few days, all the way to Baltimore or Annapolis; probably for some senators or something.

Maybe that's why the Coast Guard is hanging around so much. So how do you see it, Max?"

"I don't know yet. So far there are several people I know of with a motive to feel ill disposed towards Jack Coleman. Tom and Nell Paisley for starters, not to mention Billy Thebold."

"Billy Thebold? What did Jack Coleman ever do to him?"

"Nothing as far as I know, but if Billy were to secretly murder a man everyone knows was the subject of Tom Paisley's jealous wrath, Tom would get the blame. It would be a neat way of getting revenge on Tom and removing him from the picture all at the same time. Then Billy might have a clear field with Nell."

"Holy... Do you have any evidence about this idea, Max?"

"No, nothing as yet. It's just a possibility at this point. I'm planning on talking to Billy, though."

"Anyone else look suspicious to you?"

"I don't have any other actual names at the moment, but I'm still looking into it. By the way, do you have any information on Billy Thebold?"

"I have his last known address from a report I did at the time he was tangled up with the Paisleys. Hold on a minute. We'll stop in my office and I'll see what I got."

They pulled up in front of Sergeant Bentley's office and went inside. Bentley rummaged through some old file cabinets for a few minutes, then smiled with satisfaction.

"Here it is. He was in a rooming house on West Main near the river in Salisbury, but that was over a year ago. I heard tell he still comes into Crisfield to see Nell, but keeps his head down."

"He sounds kind of elusive," said Max. "Well, I'll look around town and keep my eyes and ears open. I could use some luck right now."

J.D. and Casper turned up in the Karen Rebecca a few minutes later. Max greeted them as they tied up at the dock.

"Hey there. Are you boys sure you want to go along with Gaston Means?"

"No we don't, Max," Casper answered, "but we're over a barrel."

"And that barrel will be heading for Niagara Falls if you give that guy any money."

"Max..."

"All right. You're both adults. I'll go with you. Just do me one favor; let me hold the money."

The Commercial Hotel looked deserted, but Gaston Means soon appeared when Max and the watermen turned up. As before, he sat on the porch and invited his guests to do the same.

"Have there been any new developments in the case?" J.D. asked.

Means folded his hands over his stomach.

"Alas, no. Mr. Smith called me last night and said he would be withdrawing his offer in a week. Coincidentally, I have to return to Washington at that time and conclude my investigation. After that, who knows?"

"Well, we raised most of the money," said Casper. "We got it in that envelope Max is holdin'."

Means looked at the envelope the way a hungry dog would look at a steak.

"Did you say *most* of the money?"

"Look. We're still tryin', Mr. Means. The bank is workin' on a loan against the boat. As it is, we got almost $2,000 together."

Means looked grim. "I don't know if Mr. Smith will accept that. He was very specific. Still, I can certainly try. Naturally, I will give you a receipt. I should be able to make contact tonight or possibly tomorrow."

He reached for the envelope, but Max made no move to give it to him.

"Before any money starts changing hands, I'd like to talk to Mr. Smith myself."

It was hard to tell who was the most surprised, the watermen or Gaston Means.

"I'm afraid that's out of the question," Means protested. "Mr. Smith was very particular about staying out of sight."

"Maybe, but he certainly couldn't protest some oversight by another agent, could he? I'll just pretend to be that agent."

"Another agent...Why that's..."

"You know, that does make sense," said Casper. "That would make it all legal-like."

Suddenly Means realized he'd been cornered. He adjusted his stance.

"All right, gentlemen. I will set up the meeting, but I would feel more confident if I could offer Mr. Smith some good faith money." He reached for the envelope again and Max withheld it again.

"He'll get good faith money when he shows a little good faith on his end," said Max in a tone that indicated the uselessness of arguing further. J.D. and Casper found themselves nodding.

Means hesitated, then smiled. "As you wish. Contact me in a day or two and we'll see what we can do."

They were a block away before J.D. spoke.

"Max, I hope to hell you know what you're doing."

Allison found the Paisley Club exactly as Max had described it. In the afternoon sun, it looked shabby and out of place somehow. Every rotted sun-bleached board and every weathered windowsill stood out like a blemish. A place like this, she thought, should only be seen at night, preferably when there was no moon.

She passed by the place casually, trying to think of a way to strike up a conversation with Nell Paisley that wouldn't set off alarm bells or get her thrown out when she heard a door open. A woman that was obviously Nell Paisley appeared, hauling out a can of trash from the night before. The woman dumped the trash in a bigger barrel and stood looking around. Allison pretended to look in a dusty store window and followed Nell Paisley in the reflection.

"Now who's the detective?" she murmured to herself.

She was about to turn around and walk over to speak with Nell Paisley, when the edge of her vision, Allison saw a young man appear.

He greeted Nell Paisley, then they looked around, squeezed behind the trash barrel and embraced. Allison's eyebrows raised, but she gave no other sign she had seen them. She went in the store and browsed slowly, keeping a lookout across the street the whole time through the shop window. Nell and the young man seemed to be on *very* good terms. Finally, the man left and started down the street. Allison slipped out of the store and followed. The streets were mostly empty. In a minute he would notice her following him. The man stopped to light a cigarette and Allison ducked into a doorway. A few seconds later she emerged and resumed following. To her relief, she saw they were traveling along Main Street, getting closer to the waterfront and to Sergeant Bentley's office.

The man turned into a doorway under a sign that said Pluck Daugherty's Pool Room. Allison kept walking past. She turned a corner and breathed a sigh of relief. Sergeant Bentley's office was only a few blocks farther.

"And that's what happened, Max," she said breathlessly. Max had just gotten back to Sergeant Bentley's office after saying goodbye to the watermen. "He turned into that pool hall at the end of the block. I think he's still there."

Max hugged her. "Good work. I believe I'd like to talk with that young Lothario. Now come with me and point him out."

Pluck Daugherty's pool room had a large window that gave a good view of the inside. Several figures bent over a table in the smoky gloom. Balls on the table rolled and clicked.

"That's him," said Allison. "The one in the blue shirt."

"All right. Now you run back to Sergeant Bentley's office and wait there. I'm going to have a little chat with our friend."

"Max, you be careful. I don't want to have to go to another séance to talk to you."

"Don't worry. Now off you go."

Allison reluctantly walked away as Max walked into the pool room. The players' heads turned and looked at him for a moment, then went back to their game. Max walked over casually and stood next to the man Allison had followed as he stood chalking his cue. Max stood looking at the table. He decided to play a hunch.

"Hello, Billy," said Max. "We need to talk."

The man looked at Max with obvious hostility. "I don't know you. What have we got to talk about?"

Max continued looking at the table. "Lighthouses."

"I got nothing to say to you, mister."

Max shrugged. "Have it your way. I'll just have to talk to someone else. I understand Police Headquarters is just up the street. Good day, Mister Thebold...and good luck. You're going to need it."

Max walked back outside slowly and deliberately. He noticed Allison was standing watch down at the street corner, ready to sound the alarm in case of trouble, bless her heart.

The door behind him opened and Billy Thebold came out, still holding his pool cue. He was about thirty and had sandy hair and a furtive expression. They stood just outside the door.

A train was pulling out, moving up the center of the street and slowly gathering speed. The noise made talking impossible for a few minutes. Finally, Billy Thebold spoke.

"All right, mister. Who are you and what do you want?"

"I'm Max Hurlock and I'm investigating the murder of Jack Coleman, the lighthouse keeper."

"So what's that got to do with me?"

"Considering how your last fling with Nell turned out, I have to admit I was surprised to hear you were coming around again. Things must be pretty serious between the two of you."

"That's none of your business, and you still haven't said what it has to do with the murder of Jack Coleman."

Max looked at the end of the train, now getting smaller as it moved away.

"Well, let's see," said Max. "We have a lighthouse keeper who's having, or trying to have an affair with Nell Paisley. You are obviously courting the lady as well. If Jack Coleman wasn't around, it would certainly make things easier for you."

Billy was unrattled. "And if President Harding had never heard of the Teapot Dome it would have made things easier for him. So what?"

"Well, I've got a suspicious mind. I can't help it. See, I figure if the lighthouse keeper should be murdered in a way that implicated Tom Paisley, that would be even better for you because you would get rid of two obstacles and get revenge on Tom Paisley at the same time. Tom goes off to jail, and you and Nell live happily ever after. Very neat."

Billy Thebold was silent a moment, then snickered with contempt.

"Some investigator. To prove murder, you have to have motive, means, and opportunity. Sounds like all you have on me is motive, and a pretty thin one at that. Last time I checked, courts prefer to have some evidence before they convict a man. When you get some, let me know. Now I agreed to talk with you out of curiosity, but I think I've wasted enough of my time. If you want to tell that tale to the cops, be my guest. I imagine they could use a good laugh."

"All right, Billy. If you're innocent as you say, why don't you give me something I can hang my hat on; something that'll help me finger the real killer. That should be easy for a man like you, a man that gets around and talks to people around here. You must have seen or heard something."

"Nuts to you. I'm not a stool pigeon."

"Suit yourself, Billy. You don't have to tell me a thing about the murder, but I am curious about one other thing."

"Just one?"

"How do you stay out of Tom Paisley's way when you're pitching woo with Nell?"

"Look. Let's get one thing straight; I'm not afraid of Tom Paisley and I'm not afraid of you. I didn't kill Jack Coleman and I wasn't part of his blackmail scheme. I'm a bookkeeper and a radio operator; I'm not a bootlegger and I'm not a cop. And since you're not a cop either, I'll be on my way. I'm not answering any more questions."

"Wait a minute," said Max, grabbing at Billy's arm, "What was that about a blackmail scheme?"

Billy pulled his arm away and sneered one more time.

"Sorry; that's a question."

And he walked away.

Chapter 15

More pieces of the puzzle

Max walked slowly back towards Sergeant Bentley's office, wondering what Billy Thebold had meant, when he heard a familiar voice.

"Max. Over here."

Max turned to see Brian Murphy behind him.

"Hello, Brian. I didn't know you came into Crisfield this often."

"It varies, depending on business. It was lucky I spotted you. I've been calling your house. I got some information for you."

"I can always use more information."

Brian Murphy lit a cigarette and looked around before continuing.

"I've been asking around like I promised and I found a runner who was near the Devil's Island light the night Jack Coleman was killed. They saw a boat there and it wasn't Jack's."

"Good work, Brian. I'm much obliged. But why hasn't this witness come forward before?"

"He's a colored boy from over in Deal. He's kept his mouth shut because he didn't want it known he was near the light that night in case some idiot Klansman might hear about it, put two and two together and get five. If certain elements around here think a black man killed Jack Coleman, they might do something stupid, so my man is cautious. But I persuaded him to talk to you."

"Thank you. I suppose he's one of your runners?"

"On occasion. Here's his address. His name is Rufus Grace. You can drop in anytime today or tomorrow. He's expectin' you."

"Thank you, Brian. You can count on my discretion."

"I know that. Otherwise, I wouldn't be helpin'."

"That and the fact that you want the case cleared up as soon as possible so things can get back to normal for your business," said Max.

Brian Murphy smiled. "Duffy Merkle was right. You are a good detective."

Encouraged by her earlier detective work, and anxious to avoid boring conversation from Sergeant Bentley, Allison ventured forth once again while Max went off in search of Rufus Grace. She was fairly sure she hadn't been noticed when she went to the Paisley Club earlier, so she decided to go again. If she could talk to Nell, it would fit in nicely with Max's questioning of Billy Thebold.

She went to the front door and stood for a moment trying to decide how best to approach Nell Paisley. The magazine article ploy seemed best. She knocked and the door opened. Instead of Nell Paisley, however, the person who emerged was husband Tom.

He was burly and coarse looking, with thick arms and at least a day's growth of beard. He was startled to see Allison, but not exactly unhappy.

"Oh. Hello. We're not open yet, Miss..."

"I didn't mean to intrude. My name is Allison Winslow." (Allison always gave her maiden name when she didn't want someone to know her relationship with Max.) "I'm visiting Crisfield looking for material for a magazine article I'm writing. I was hoping to see what a local, er, club looked like, and someone said the Paisley Club was the best in town."

Tom Paisley smiled in what he apparently thought was a charming manner. "Well, then why not come inside and take a look?"

Allison hesitated. "Well..."

"Come on. I don't bite."

Allison walked in, fingering the stiff hatpin she wore in case of emergencies. The inside was as dark as Max had told her, but there was no sign of Nell. Drat.

"Well, this is the club," said Tom, gesturing around the room with his arm. "What do you think?"

"Charming. Do you have a business partner, Mr. Paisley?"

"My wife, Nell. That's it. I have several employees; bartenders, waiters and the like."

"Is she around?"

"Nell? No. She ran out on an errand." He moved slightly closer. Allison backed up toward the door, pulling out her hatpin and palming it just in case.

"Tell me, Mr. Paisley; do you serve alcohol here?"

"Not officially, but we do make exceptions."

"If you were to serve alcohol, where would you get it; what with Prohibition and all?"

He chuckled. "That's no problem around here. Bootleggers are thinker than fleas on a hound dog. Every back creek is a liquor route." He inched closer.

"I read there was a murder out at a lighthouse recently. Do you think that had anything to do with rum running?"

"Maybe, but that's not my problem," he said. "Say, why do you want to know about liquor? Just what magazine article are you writing, anyway?"

His smile faded and his voice now had an undertone of suspicion. He stepped closer as Allison backed away.

"I like to get local background when I write. You know; news, rumors and the like."

"Uh huh." His voice was suddenly friendly again, too friendly for Allison's taste. His smile was back and was becoming a leer.

"My, you are a pretty thing, aren't you? Maybe you'd like a little drink while you're here? You can sample the quality of our wares; see what the local distillers have to offer. They're doing some great things with fermented corn these days. Why don't you slide on over to the bar there and old Tom'll see what he can do."

Allison's back was against the front door now. She felt around behind her for the knob but couldn't find it. He leaned in toward her. His breath smelled stale.

"I'm sorry. I really must be going," she said firmly. "I'm meeting someone. She'll come looking for me."

"Then we'll invite her in and we'll have us a party."

Allison swallowed. She grasped the hatpin like a knife, and braced herself. A quick knee to the groin and a thrust with the hatpin should take the starch out of Tom Paisley in a hurry...she hoped.

"Mr. Paisley, I really must be going. Now, I'm going to ask you one more time: please stand back and let me leave."

No answer, just more leering and leaning. She drew her arm back to strike. Sorry, buddy, she thought, but you asked for it...

"Tom! What are you doing?"

The voice of Nell filled the room with outrage.

"I leave for five minutes and you bring some floozy in here? Damn you, Tom!"

"Floozy?" said Allison under her breath.

Tom turned to engage a very angry Nell. Allison quietly slid the hatpin back in place.

"This lady is writing a magazine article and she wanted to see the club. I was just showing her around; you know; showing some hospitality."

"By pinning her to the wall? I wasn't born yesterday, you palooka! So help me Tom, this is the last straw. I'm sick of you running around."

Allison felt no inclination to come to Tom's defense. She just stood still taking in the remarkable show as Tom and Nell squared off in the dingy speakeasy shouting and waving their arms in a way they had no doubt done more than once before. Although her presence had started the fight, they seemed to have forgotten she was there.

"If I didn't have a half interest in this place, I'd leave you."

At this, Tom changed his strategy from denial to counterattack. "Oh, really? And do what? Run off with that Billy Thebold creep?"

"Don't you bring up Billy Thebold, you lug. I haven't seen him in ages. Besides, he's a perfect gentleman. He's not like you at all."

"I'll say he isn't," Tom retorted. "That little backstabbing twerp doesn't own half of this club!"

After a few more minutes of this, Allison slipped out the front door into the sunlight. Neither Tom Paisley nor his wife noticed her leave.

"Whew! Now there's a match made in heaven. It's a good thing Nell Paisley didn't have the hatpin."

Sergeant Bentley had loaned Max his Model T for the short trip to Deal. Max followed the directions and soon came to a gray wooden mailbox with faded letters that said Grace. A twisted dirt driveway led to several shacks and a weedy yard piled with ropes, crab traps, oyster tongs, a rusty anchor, and an old automobile jacked up with a wheel missing. Several children played in the yard and looked at Max curiously. On one side of the yard a heavy set black woman was hanging laundry on a sagging clothesline. She looked at Max and called for Rufus. Presently a tall thin black man appeared, wiping his hands on a greasy rag.

"Mr. Grace? I'm Max Hurlock. I think Brian Murphy told you I would be stopping by."

Rufus Grace wasn't used to white men calling him Mr. Grace, and he looked at Max warily. Then he nodded and motioned for Max to follow him into the shack. Inside, the place was clean but shabby. A wood stove in the kitchen and an old ice box seemed to be the only appliances except for what looked like a brand new console radio in the parlor. Several walls had been wallpapered with old newspapers. On one wall was a photograph of the Grace family and on the other hung a much-reproduced portrait of Jesus in a frame that said "Mount Pleasant AME Church, Crisfield".

"Brian Murphy tells me you were in the vicinity of the Devil's Elbow light the night the keeper was murdered," said Max.

"That's right. I was makin' a delivery for Mr. Murphy, long 'bout nine or so."

"And you saw a boat at the light?"

"That's right."

"What kind of boat?"

"Looked like a Hooper Island Draketail. That's a long narrow workboat with…"

Max held up a hand. "I'm familiar with Draketails. Did you see any people?"

"No."

"Was the light on?"

"The light was on and the station was lit up."

"Anything unusual about this boat? Anything you could use to identify it?"

"No. It was pretty dark and I was maybe a hundred yards away. Couldn't see no name on the stern."

"You said you were making a delivery. Was the boat still there when you came back?"

"No, and the light was out."

"And that was around…"

"Eleven."

"Have you noticed any other strange boats at that light at night in the past few weeks?"

"Nope. Just the keeper's boat."

"I guess that's all I need," said Max, rising from his chair. "Say, while I'm here, could I see your boat?"

For the first time, Rufus Grace smiled. He led Max out the back door. On the way out, Max noticed a brown envelope on the kitchen table. Sticking out of the envelope was stack of ten dollar bills. Between that and the new radio, Rumrunning must be very profitable, Max thought.

The Grace property was on a shallow creek that led to the bay. A rickety boathouse, gray with age, stood on an equally rickety pier. Rufus led Max inside where in the dim light, a workboat bobbed. From the lines, Max could see that it would hold a lot of bootleg liquor. The hatch cover was thrown back revealing an engine that seemed familiar.

"Is that an engine from an airplane?" said Max, astonished.

Rufus Grace's face lit up with pride. "That's right, Mr. Max, a 90 horsepower Curtiss Wright OX-5 out of a Curtis Jenny airplane. One of 'em crashed near here and I bought the engine off the owner real cheap. I worked on it 'till it purred like a kitten. Me and my cousin mounted it in this old work boat and now we got us one of the fastest runners on the bay."

Max examined the engine with fascination. "You seem to have way with machinery. I'll bet you could give the Coast Guard a fit."

"Want to hear her run?"

"You bet."

Rufus Grace started the motor and Max admired the smooth rumble of power. If only Gypsy could run this well.

"It's pretty quiet," Max remarked.

"I rigged up mufflers on the exhaust," said Rufus. "No sense advertisin' where you be at night. Now listen to this. I put extra insulation in the engine housing."

He closed the engine cover and Max was amazed how quiet the engine became. Maybe this helped to explain how the "disappearing rum runner" was so elusive at night. He looked in the small forward cabin.

"I see you have a two-way radio."

"We keep in touch with Mr. Murphy in case there's trouble. He's got a radio set up somewhere north of Crisfield. Sometimes, if we're takin' a load off a rum ship, we get signals from them, too."

Max nodded, and noticed a notebook by the radio.

"What's this?" he asked. "It almost looks like..."

"It's a codebook. If we gotta talk on the radio, we can't just go around blabbing in the clear. The Coast Guard'd be all over us. We use a code. Like Mr. Murphy says, a business man has to take precautions."

Max nodded with satisfaction. He had come seeking one piece of the puzzle. Perhaps he had stumbled on another one.

Max returned Sergeant Bentley's car and heard Allison's story. He was not happy.

"You know, I'm really getting fed up with Tom Paisley's shenanigans. First he gives me the brush off, then he tries to move in on my wife."

"He didn't know I was your wife, Max. I used the Allison Winslow wheeze on him."

"And that makes it all right?"

"Well, it makes it less personal, at least. Look, I was able to find out that Tom doesn't know that Billy Thebold is still seeing Nell and that they seem to cheat on each other constantly."

"And what do you conclude from all of that?"

"I conclude," said Allison, "that Billy Thebold had better hope Tom never finds out."

"And I found out that an unknown Hooper Island Draketail was at the light the night Jack Coleman was killed, but that doesn't seem to get us much closer to a solution."

"Yes," said Allison, "and J.D. and Casper only have a few days before Gaston Means files a report saying they killed Jack Coleman."

"Well, tomorrow we go to Baltimore," said Max. "Maybe I'll find out something helpful there when I talk to the Coast Guard, the Lighthouse Service and the Sunpapers reporter."

John Reisinger

Chapter 16

Steamboat to Baltimore

The steamship dock at Claiborne the next morning was a madhouse of milling passengers, stacks of luggage, barrels of fish, bushels of crabs, and wooden crates of who-knows-what awaiting transport to Baltimore. The crowd streamed onto the boat, filling the decks and the interior spaces, with black passengers relegated to the stern and the fantail, and white passengers everywhere else. Some were traveling on business and some were returning from excursions to Ocean City.

The steamboat Cambridge was a lumbering white floating mansion, or at least, that's the way it had always appeared to Allison. The brass rails, the long promenade deck, the curtained smoking room and the rich, wood paneled saloon reminded her of an exclusive private club where money is no object.

Max held a less romantic view.

"Look at the smoke from that stack," he said, looking upward and shading his eyes. "It's way too black. They need to open the dampers and let more air get to the boiler fires."

Allison held her hat on against the wind. "Now, Max. Maybe you should let the crew drive the boat."

"You don't drive a boat, you..."

His words were lost in the long piercing scream of the steam whistle as the Cambridge slowly pulled away from the dock in Claiborne.

"We're off, Max. Isn't it exciting?"

He slid his arm around her waist and pulled her close. "Now that you mention it..."

The Cambridge headed westerly, then turned north at Bloody Point Bar light. The rougher waters of the Chesapeake caused a gentle roll as the steamboat pushed up the bay.

Max and Allison stood by the rail and breathed deeply. A few seagulls wheeled overhead and astern, looking for small fish churned up in the steamship's wake, and there were scores of white workboats scattered around the water tonging and dredging for oysters,

"Do you suppose J.D. and Casper are in one of those boats, Max?"

"I doubt it. They usually work further south, towards Tilghman Island and the Choptank; maybe even Crisfield, although that town might not be so attractive to them just now."

"I suppose not. Do you really think this Gaston Means character is trying to wheedle the money out of them? Maybe there really is a mysterious informant."

"Maybe there really is a Santa Claus, but I'm not betting on it. No, I think Sergeant Bentley had Means pegged; a grifter in a ten dollar suit."

"Well, I have faith in you, Max. Maybe you'll find out something from the Coast Guard or the Sunpaper office in Baltimore."

"I hope so. I can't get the bigger picture by just knocking around in Crisfield. Anyway, what's your schedule? Do you want to go see Houdini perform at the Hippodrome tonight?"

"We can't. His first Baltimore performance isn't until tomorrow, so we'll have to wait until then. I have another plan for tonight."

"Does it involve a romantic evening at the Belvedere Hotel?"

"At the end of the night, yes. First, however, we're going to a séance."

"Another séance? You mean you didn't get your fill the first time?"

"This is different. This séance is conducted by Irene Sterling, Baltimore's leading medium. Isis Dalrymple tells me she was Madame DeSousa's mentor and I thought it would be interesting to see if she has the same bag of tricks, assuming that they really are tricks."

"Don't tell me you're starting to believe all that hocus pocus?"

"Not on an intellectual level, Max, but I'm having a hard time rationalizing what I saw that night. I know Madame DeSousa didn't do those tricks and I know her assistant didn't either, so what gives?"

Max shrugged. "Maybe that's why they call it the unexplained."

"Maybe I'll have better luck with Irene Sterling."

"And you want me to go?"

"Oh, yes, Max. I want to hear your impression of what you see tonight. Maybe there's an engineering explanation."

"Great. Now I have two mysteries I can't solve."

Three hours later the Cambridge was in Baltimore. In the harbor approaches, they had passed Fort Carroll, whose construction had been supervised by Robert E. Lee, and then Fort McHenry, the inspiration for the writing of the Star Spangled Banner, the music that was played when the flag was raised on military posts.

The Cambridge pulled in at the Light Street steamship terminal, squeezing in among a row of similar vessels and another scene of chaos ensued as passengers getting off the steamship competed with passengers getting on for the return trip to Claiborne. On Light Street, traffic picking up or dropping off people at the steamship terminal competed with horse drawn carts and motor trucks moving products and other cargo from the boats. Although the skies were clear, the street was wet and spotted with puddles. Boxes and barrels were stacked in pyramids along the street and people seemed to be everywhere. The air was a heady mixture of the smells of coal smoke, fish, garbage, and horse manure.

"Well, this place is pretty much as I remembered it," said Allison.

"Let's get up to the hotel and get settled," said Max. I have a few hours to check with the Coast Guard before dinner.

"Just don't be late getting back," Allison reminded him. "Remember, my father is picking us up at five thirty and bringing us back for dinner in Roland Park."

The Belvedere Hotel was on a hill on Charles Street, not too far from Mt Vernon Place. As Max and Allison entered the lobby, they saw a small English pub-like room off to the left. Although it was early, the place was busy.

"Now here we have an example of Prohibition in action," said Allison. "My father told me about this. Let's have a look."

A small sign announced the room was called the Owl Bar. It was done in dark wood, and had tables with checkered tablecloths. True to its name, the Owl Bar had a full size plaster owl over the bar looking on the proceedings. What was most remarkable, though, was the owl's eyes, two eerily glowing red lights.

"Baltimore is casual about enforcing Prohibition," Allison explained, "so this place often serves alcohol openly. Even so, sometimes a zealous agent will come sniffing around and it won't be safe. When that happens, the owl's eyes will flash on and off, warning the patrons not to show or ask for liquor."

Max shook his head. "One thing you have to say for Prohibition; it sure brings out people's creative side."

After they had checked into their room, Allison strolled off to the Enoch Pratt Library, a stone building many out of towners mistook for a railway station, and Max went off to talk to the Coast Guard.

The Coast Guard Station at Curtis Bay, just south of the city was a depot for ship repair as well as a base for operations. Max had set up an appointment with Lieutenant Scheffel and was ushered into his office overlooking the piers. Scheffel was almost bald and wore a white shirt with a dark tie. His jacket, with two gold stripes on the sleeve, was hanging on the wall.

"So you want to know about the rum war, eh?" said Scheffel without waiting for an introduction. "Well, I'll tell you about it in two words; we're losing. We don't have enough people, enough boats, or enough time to properly patrol. About the only thing we have plenty of is rumrunners and empty water. The Coast Guard is the country's oldest seagoing service; older than the Navy. We have a proud tradition, but now we're reduced to chasing floating liquor stores."

"It must be frustrating," said Max.

"We're in a recruiting drive to man some of the new boats, but we've lowered standards to fill the billets. So now they call us the Dry Navy or the Hooligan Navy."

Max stifled a smile. He had heard the terms before. "I'm investigating the death of the lighthouse keeper at the Devil's Elbow light. I wondered if any of your boats might have been in the area and maybe saw or heard of anything suspicious that might shed some light on what happened."

Scheffel settled down and thought for a moment, then started shuffling through a pile of reports on his desk.

"I think the CG-182 was in the area on night patrol. As I recall, they investigated because they noticed the light was out." He called for the yeoman in the outside office.

"Bellini, how about getting me the report from the 182 for the night that lighthouse keeper was killed."

He turned back to Max. "Yes, we're trying to sweep the ocean with a broom, but orders are orders. I can't even estimate the number that slip through. It's almost as if someone is tipping them off. Sometimes they coordinate with radios using coded messages."

"Can you track the location of the radios?" Max asked.

"We try, but they keep the transmissions short and our radio direction finding equipment needs time to get a good fix. Even then, we're using our moving boats to find the location of a radio on one of their moving boats, so even if we do get a location, it's only good to within a couple of miles, so it's useless. It's like a fox hunt with a hundred foxes and only four or five hounds. Ah, here we are."

The yeoman had dropped the report on his desk and he read it carefully.

"As I thought. Chief Voshel reported the light out at 0120. He approached the light to investigate and found the entire station was dark."

"Someone else said the light was on earlier," said Max.

"There was one boat at the light, a skiff. Maybe twenty foot long and slung on the davits."

"That's the light keeper's boat," said Max. "The visitor's boat must have been long gone by then. Did they board the lighthouse?"

"No. They notified the Lighthouse Service by radio. The lighthouse boys said they'd call the keeper and investigate."

"But the radio was disconnected by then."

Scheffel thumbed through the report. "I can't say. The Lighthouse Service didn't respond further. Chief Voshel reported back to base and recommended a Notice to Mariners be issued warning the light was out temporarily, and that was all we have."

"Hmm. Mr. Scheffel, did they stop any possible runners that night?"

The papers shuffled again. Yes. Looks like five of them, but none were carrying any contraband."

"Then what were they doing out at that time of night?"

"Three said they'd been fishing on the other shore; one said he'd had engine trouble and was late getting back and the other said he was visiting a sick friend on the other side. Some of them probably were running bootleg, but dumped it when they saw us coming. Of course, if they could dump it that fast, they weren't carrying all that much, so we're not worried about it. It's the big shipments moving at night we look out for."

"Anything else happen that night?"

Lieutenant Scheffel looked again. "Hmmm. It looks like they ran into the disappearing runner again."

"The disappearing runner? I heard someone mention that. What's the story?"

"We've seen it several times, always at night. It's hard to pick out a low slung boat running without lights at night, but sometimes we can pick up a silhouette. Then we...say, there's Chief Voshel now. Hey, Chief; how about stopping in for a minute."

Max recognized the chief of the CG-182 he had talked to when the Karen Rebecca was stopped. They exchanged greetings.

"Chief, tell Mr. Hurlock here about our latest encounter with the disappearing runner."

Voshel snorted. "It's like chasing the great white whale, only harder to see. It's always the same. We spot a low silhouette of a boat at night and set a course to intercept. When we get close enough, we turn on our searchlight and challenge it. But this runner always vanishes before we get near it. There is a sudden flash of bright light, and the boat is gone. We increase speed if we can, but it never makes any difference. The boat has disappeared. It's happened four times so far."

"A pretty good mystery in its own right," said Max, "but I'm not sure if it has anything to do with my case. Could I look through the reports from a month or so before the death of the lighthouse keeper?"

Scheffel nodded. "Sure thing. I'll have Benelli get them for you. You can use the small conference room down the hall."

"Thank you. So, do either of you have any opinion on the death of the lighthouse keeper?"

Scheffel and the chief both shook their heads.

"I don't know Mr. Hurlock," said Scheffel, "but after everything I've seen in the last few years around here, nothing would surprise me."

Max thanked him and started looking through the patrol reports of the past few weeks, not knowing exactly what he was looking for. Most were routine stops, so he concentrated on the ones late at night, figuring anyone out on the bay that late must be up to something. He looked through page after page of the same routine of stop and search, with only a few yielding contraband liquor.

Suddenly Max stopped. Three weeks earlier, a smaller Coast Guard patrol boat had stopped a suspicious boat a little after midnight traveling without lights near the Devil's Elbow light. There were five men on board who claimed they were doing night fishing. The boat had a false panel concealing a hidden storage area, but no liquor was found. Among the five names were two he recognized; J.D. Pratt and Casper Nowitsky.

At the Enoch Pratt library, Allison looked through the Baltimore Sun newspaper files for the past year for anything involving spiritualism. She found several articles about Arthur Conan Doyle and his firm belief in communicating with the dead. At one point, Doyle claimed the spirit of his dead son Kingsley massaged his injured leg. He believed there was no other explanation for the phenomena he witnessed at séances and the messages he received from his deceased wife and son. In light of what she witnessed at Madame DeSousa's, Allison knew just how he felt. The séance that night at Irene Sterling's might prove to be very interesting.

John Reisinger

Chapter 17

The mysterious Mr. Collins

Max got back to the hotel just in time to change for dinner, and get to the curb outside the Belvedere Hotel with Allison.

"Glad you could make it, Max. My father will be here in five minutes."

"Ah, yes. The good Dr. Osgood Winslow. I can't wait for his latest medical story."

"Now, Max. Daddy just likes to talk shop once in a while."

"Yes; every time I show up."

"He respects your intellect, Max. You should be flattered."

"Yes, nothing goes with a fine dinner like a wide ranging discussion on the vicissitudes of the human pancreas. Can't he find someone to regale down at Johns Hopkins?"

"Never mind that. What did you find out from the *Semper Paratus* boys?"

"The Devil's Elbow light was out at 1:20 AM and they encountered a rumrunner that seemed to vanish into thin air."

"More spirits up to mischief?"

"Mischief, yes, but I think the only spirits were stowed in the hold. Anyway, there was another odd thing; J.D. and Casper were stopped on a boat set up for rumrunning one night a few weeks ago."

"So your down home pals have a secret life?"

"I don't know what to think. Maybe they had just borrowed the boat, maybe..."

"Hush up. Here's daddy to pick us up."

A Packard pulled up to the curb and the Hurlocks climbed in and set off for dinner at the Winslows'.

Allison's girlhood home was a large shingled house set in a heavily wooded lot into the side of a hill along Deepdene Road in Baltimore's Roland Park.

"How can people live on such uneven ground?" Max always said, being used to the flatness of the Eastern Shore. "I mean, if you stumble in your front yard, you're likely to roll down to the end of the block."

Seated around the dinner table a short while later, Allison's father, Dr. Osgood Winslow began one of his medical stories. Dr. Winslow wore a pair of Benjamin Franklin glasses that he was constantly taking off, polishing, and putting back on. He was also completely bald, giving his head the appearance of some pink egg that had somehow learned to talk.

"Then there was old Bob Simon," he began. "He was a good doctor, but not always as alert as he should have been. I remember one day, he was all ready to recommend drastic treatment to a patient with a very faint heartbeat. He thought the man was dying because his heart was so weak he could barely hear it. Come to find out, the patient simply had a case of *Situs Inversus.*"

Max was the only one at the table not laughing, including Allison's mother.

"Don't you get it, Max?" said Allison helpfully. "*Situs Inversus*; the reversal of the thoracic and abdominal organs. The heart would be on the other side of the chest, so the heartbeat would sound faint if the stethoscope were applied in the usual spot."

"Oh yes," said Max. "That was going to be my next guess. That was a real knee-slapper. I'll have to tell that one to J.D. and Casper. They'll be rolling on the ground laughing."

"I suppose the lesson here," Dr. Winslow continued, "is the danger of making assumptions. They can lead you astray."

"Amen to that," said Max. "As Mark Twain said, it's not what you don't know that gets you in trouble, it's what you do know that turns out to be wrong."

"All right, Osgood," said Allison's mother Beatrice. "That's enough of your stories for now. Let's hear what Allison and Max have been up to. I understand you're both going to a séance tonight?"

"Yes, mother," said Allison, "at Irene Sterling's. It starts at eight and it's only about three blocks away."

"Seances? In Roland Park? Bah! A lot of nonsense." Dr. Winslow was back in the thick of the conversation again.

"Now, Osgood...," said Allison's mother patiently. "I don't want you off on one of your opinion explosions again."

"Why do you say séances are nonsense?" said Allison.

He took his glasses off again. "Allison, I've seen plenty of dead people in my career and if there's one thing I'm sure of, it's this; you can talk to the dead all you want, but only a fool would expect them to talk back."

Irene Sterling's house was on Upland Road, another quiet tree-lined street a few blocks from the Winslows'. From a large, pillared front porch, Max and Allison were ushered into a spacious, tall-ceilinged parlor decorated in heavy furniture and dark colors similar to Madame DeSousa's.

"The medium business must be booming," said Max under his breath.

"Let's split up until it starts," said Allison. "That way we can each talk to people and get their impressions."

Max drifted over to an elderly woman, who was nervously twisting her handkerchief.

"Hello. Have you been to a séance before?"

"The woman jumped as if startled. "Uh, no. This is my first. I really don't know why I came. It's just that I lost my husband last year and...well, I thought that maybe..."

"I understand," said Max. "Hope is a powerful thing."

She looked at him wistfully. "Yes, it certainly is, isn't it?"

In another corner of the room, Allison spotted a quiet man who sat on a sofa and kept to himself. He was wearing a coat and a fedora. The man had thick black hair poking out from beneath his hat and wore a pair of large heavy glasses. He looked lost.

Allison sat next to him and said hello. The man simply nodded politely.

"My name is Allison Hurlock."

"Samuel Collins." The man's voice was scratchy and hoarse. He spoke slowly and had an accent that sounded vaguely Eastern European.

"I'm really excited to be here. Have you been to a séance before, Mr. Collins?"

"Yes. Several."

There was another awkward silence. Mr. Collins seemed to be self-conscious about being there. Allison decided to give it one more try.

"Actually, I'm here doing research for a magazine article on spiritualism I'm writing."

Mr. Collins suddenly seemed interested.

"Really? Have you written magazine articles before?"

"Oh, yes. My work has appeared in Southern Times, Modern Girls, Archer's Monthly and several others."

"Very impressive. And have you formed any conclusions about spiritualism, Miss Hurlock?"

"To tell you the truth, I'm very skeptical. I mean the whole concept doesn't make sense to me, and I know many mediums have been exposed as fakes by Houdini and others, but I've seen things at a recent séance that I can't explain." She relayed the happenings at Madame DeSousa's.

Mr. Collins nodded. "Some mediums produce very convincing phenomena. That is what convinced Conan Doyle, I understand."

"Yes, I've read about that. But I want to look beyond the surface and see what lies beneath. I want to look beyond people's assumptions."

"A good approach. I see they are calling us to the table. Perhaps we should sit together Miss Hurlock. I find your attitude refreshing, so we may both find the evening illuminating."

"You're on, Mr. Collins."

Allison took a place at the large table with Mr. Collins on her left, and Max on her right. Next to Max was the woman he had been talking to, who seemed to have gotten over her shyness completely. Introductions were made and the lights dimmed.

Irene Sterling appeared in much the same way Madame DeSousa had. She greeted the guests and talked about the spirits and proper decorum. Then she sat down and instructed everyone to hold hands. Everyone did and the lights went out.

"I have to scratch my nose," whispered Mr. Collins. He withdrew his hand for a second, then grasped Allison's hand again with a whispered apology and the séance was on.

Madame DeSousa had given an impressive séance, but Irene Sterling seemed to have a direct connection to the afterlife. Spirits appeared, then vanished. The table rose and settled back. The table light glowed, then went dark. Voices came and went, and the air seemed to dance with glowing trumpets, tambourines and even a violin. Mr. Collins asked about a departed friend and was assured by the friend's spirit he was well and happy. Others talked to deceased relatives, loved ones and friends. The effect was dazzling and overpowering, almost sensory overload.

"A pretty impressive show, I have to admit," whispered Max, who could feel the lady next to him squeezing his hand almost painfully.

"Max, this is overwhelming. I almost feel faint. I may have to leave," Allison whispered. Max could hear the near panic in her voice.

"Steady, old girl. Nobody ever got hurt at a séance."

"Yes, but..."

"Stop the séance!" someone shouted. The words shattered the solemn atmosphere like thunder. Allison looked around and in the dim light was shocked to see Mr. Collins was standing up and pointing at Irene Sterling...but Allison was somehow still holding his hand! What was going on?

"Stop the séance," Mr. Collins repeated. His voice was different now; strong, clear and commanding. He looked different as well; his glasses were gone and his black hair was now a lighter color.

"I am Houdini, and you, Madame, are a fraud!"

Everyone gasped and started talking at once. The lights came up and Allison was startled to see that she had not been holding Mr. Collins's hand, but the hand of the person who had been sitting on the other side of Mr. Collins. How was that possible?

"Get out of my house!" Irene Sterling shrieked. "Get out now!"

"She had addressed the remark to Mr. Collins, or whoever he was, but everyone seemed to be thinking along those lines already, and the house quickly emptied as confused patrons streamed out and disappeared into the night.

"Come on Allison," said Max, grabbing her arm. "I'm not sure what's going on, but it's no place for you."

A minute later, they found themselves standing on the sidewalk under a streetlight.

"Do you think that was really Houdini?" Allison asked.

"I don't know. He could have been a fake as well. One thing is for sure, though; he brought down the house."

"Well, now what?" asked Allison.

"This is your old neighborhood," said Max. "How do we get back to the Belvedere?"

"If we go up this road, we'll come to Roland Avenue. We can catch a streetcar from there."

"Let's get started then."

"Miss Hurlock!"

They turned to see Mr. Collins approaching. As he came into the light of the street lamp, Allison got a good look at his face, now without the glasses, hat and wig. His hair, parted in the middle, was dark and curly, with gray at the temples, and his eyes were penetrating, almost hypnotic. Allison realized this was the face she has seen on scores of newspapers and posters.

"Jeepers!" she said to Max. "It really is Houdini!"

The man bowed slightly. "At your service. You must be Allison's husband."

"That's right. Max is the name. It's an honor."

"Allison, I wanted to catch up with you and talk about your article. I hope you will tell about what happened here tonight." Houdini spoke slowly and deliberately, enunciating each word, and with a slight accent from his native Hungary

"Uh...well, Mr. Houdini. To tell you the truth, I'm not really sure what happened. Irene Sterling is a fraud? How do you know?"

"Is there some place nearby we could go to talk?"

"Yes, I think Morgan Millard is still open up on Roland Avenue. It's about two blocks from here."

"It sounds like a law firm," Houdini observed.

"Morgan Millard Pharmacy. I've been going there for years," said Allison. "It's a half-timbered building that looks like it belongs in England. You probably passed it on your way here."

"Splendid," said Houdini, rubbing his hands together, "We'll have a little chat about the spirit world in a place worthy of Henry the Eighth."

A few minutes later, they were seated in a booth in a corner over cups of coffee. Houdini had replaced his heavy glasses so no one would recognize him. He made a quick telephone call to one of his stagehands to bring a car for him, then joined Max and Allison. As Houdini picked up his coffee, Max noticed how quick and nimble his fingers were.

"I open tomorrow night, so I got to town a day early to investigate Irene Sterling. As you may have read, I've been investigating mediums all over."

"So how do you know Irene Sterling is a fake?" Max asked.

"Two ways," Houdini answered. "I have several friends who passed away in the last few years who had a similar interest in the possibilities of an afterlife. Before they died, we agreed on certain code words we would use to authenticate any supposed spirit communication should one of us die. Although Irene Sterling claimed to be in contact with one of them, she never came up with any of the code words. My other reason is more basic; Irene Sterling's so-called manifestations were cheap conjuring tricks."

"They looked pretty convincing to me," said Allison.

Houdini chuckled. "We'll talk about that later. I was interested in the article you are doing, Mrs. Hurlock. Tell me more about it."

"Well, as I said, I am looking into spiritualism and I have a lot of trouble taking it seriously, but then I find myself face to face with things I can't explain. I told you about my experiences with Madame DeSousa. The problem is that I don't know how Madame DeSousa knew so much about me without my telling her, then caused the manifestations I saw at her séance."

"Not to mention the ones we saw tonight," Max added. "You said they were conjuring tricks. How were they done?"

"Illusions," Houdini replied. "Illusion is the stock and trade of every magician that has ever lived. Making people believe something that is not so is surprisingly easy. In my act, I have a trick where I stand on one side of a solid brick wall and announce I will pass through it. There is a large carpet underneath the wall so there is no question of me going through a trap door in the stage. A curtain is put in place to hide me from the audience, but the top of the wall remains in plain sight, so I can't get over it, either. The curtain is removed a minute later and I am on the other side of the wall. Conan Doyle firmly believes I dematerialize and actually pass through the wall. Do you think he's right?"

"Well...no...I suppose not..." Allison did not sound sure.

"You are correct. It's not magic at all, simply a trick, and a very simple one at that. There is no real magic, only illusions and showmanship. Magic depends on two things; misdirection and assumptions. Misdirection is getting the audience looking at your right hand while you are doing something you don't want them to see with your left. As for assumptions, that is simply depending on the fact that people will accept the obvious explanation without considering alternatives."

"Allison's father was talking about assumptions earlier," said Max. "He was telling us the pitfalls of taking things for granted."

Houdini smiled. "Yes. People make assumptions to fill in the blanks, so to speak. It's the way the human mind is built to avoid overload. If you are walking in the dark, you don't stop to examine every place you will put your foot. You assume the road will continue and you will not fall off a cliff. If people see a trumpet floating in the air, they assume nothing is holding it there because they can't see how it's done, but they are wrong. An assistant uses a simple fishing rod and line to produce the effect. The instruments are painted with luminous paint to glow in the dark, while the rod is painted black so it cannot be seen. The ectoplasm is thin cloth or surgical gauze. Needless to say, the assistant who circulates in the dark with a fishing rod can also place his hand on someone's shoulder or produce sound effects when required."

"Wait," said Allison. "At Madame DeSousa's and at the séance tonight, the assistant was holding hands around the table with the rest of us the entire time."

"So was I, if you recall," said Houdini with a mischievous smile. His eyes seemed to twinkle.

Allison snapped her fingers. "That's right, you were, but when the lights came up, I was holding hands with the person next to you. How did you do that?"

"Another simple trick. In the dark I remove my hand for a second to 'scratch my nose', then guide your left hand to my other neighbor's right hand, and vice-versa. You grasp the neighbor's hand and *assume* it is mine. The neighbor does the same, but I am now free to walk about in the dark while the two of you hold each other's hands. The assistant uses the same trick."

"What about the rising table?"

"A lever or switch operated by the medium's foot. The dimming light works that way as well."

"No. That can't be," Allison insisted. "At Madame DeSousa's, I had my foot on hers the whole time."

Houdini shook his head. "You had your foot on her shoe. Many mediums use a heavy stiff shoe with an open heel. While you have your foot on the shoe, they slip their foot out of the rear of the shoe to operate the switches under the table."

"And how did she know so much about me without my telling her?" said Allison.

"Some mediums do research ahead of time, or have an assistant engage customers in casual conversation ahead of time to gain information. What you experienced, however, is called a cold reading. The medium essentially keeps guessing and then follows up when he guesses correctly. You tend to remember the parts they guess right and forget the ones they get wrong."

"Assumptions again?" said Max.

"Exactly."

"So, Madame DeSousa is a fake?" said Allison.

"I'm afraid it appears that way," said Houdini with a sigh, "but don't feel badly. I have been searching for a genuine medium since my dear mother died and I have yet to find one."

"If I could ask a less spiritual question," Max began, "I am an investigator and I have a case where a rumrunner boat on the Chesapeake Bay at night disappears each time the Coast Guard closes in on it. One minute it's there, then there is a bright flash of light and it's gone. Do you have any idea how they would do that?"

Houdini thought for a moment. "I can think of several ways and they all involve misdirection and assumptions. The bright flash of light is the key. Think upon the matter and it will become clear to you as well. But I'm afraid I must be going. My automobile will be here to pick me up shortly. I must get back to write up my notes on tonight, and to prepare for my show tomorrow night."

"We have tickets for that show," said Allison.

"Excellent. Then I shall see you both again."

He shook Max's hand and turned to Allison.

"Allison, you and Max are both open-minded yet skeptical. These are good qualities. Here is my card. Please let me know when your article is published. I shall read it with great interest."

"Thank you," said Allison. "May I mention our meeting tonight, and what we discussed?"

Houdini stood up and smiled. "I would be disappointed if you did not. After all, it is free publicity, the life blood of every magician! Just make sure you read the note at the bottom of the menu there. You will find it most informative."

He pointed to the menus lying on the other side of the booth. Max and Allison each picked up a menu and looked to see what he meant. At the bottom of each menu was a handwritten note:

Beware of misdirection and assumption

Max frowned and turned back to Houdini.
"I didn't see you write any…"
But Houdini was gone.
They looked at each other. "Well, Max, I think we just got a lesson in misdirection and assumption, and we got it from the master himself."

John Reisinger

Chapter 18

News men

The next day Allison met her mother for lunch and Max went the Sunpapers offices on Calvert Street to look at the old clipping files. Most of the bigger newspapers kept files of their older stories by having someone painstakingly cut out each article and put it in a file based on the subject matter. The mysterious death of the lighthouse keeper had ten articles, all under the byline of Hal Marks.

Max ran through the articles and found some details he had missed. Gaston Means was talking about the progress he was making and all sorts of crazy rumors were circulating. Many of the theories floating around Crisfield were far-fetched, but Max made a note of them anyway.

It looked like Marks had done some digging that might help in some way.

"Humph," came a voice behind him. "The lighthouse keeper. Are you a relative?"

Max looked around and saw a short stocky man with his hair parted in the middle standing with his thumbs hooked on his suspenders.

"Er, no. I'm not a relative," said Max.

"Police?"

"No, I'm…"

"Not a clergyman?"

"No."

"Thank God for that. I hope you are not a Prohibitionist. I haven't met one yet I'd care to have a drink with."

"I'm an investigator and I'm trying to keep Gaston Means from accusing the wrong man."

"Bah. More Prohibition idiocy, I'll wager. It'll probably come down to some squabble between rumrunners. Sometimes I wonder if the apes aren't embarrassed to have common ancestors with the human race. Wait. Did you say Gaston Means?"

"Yes. Do you know him?"

"I never met the man, which is no doubt fortunate for both of us, but from what I hear, if you ever shake hands with him, you'd better count your fingers afterwards."

Max nodded. "That was my impression as well. Are you a reporter here?"

"More of a writer of editorials and opinion pieces."

"You must be good at it," said Max. "You seem to have opinions to spare."

"Well, what of it? A man with no opinions is a man with no soul. The problem is when people mistake their opinion for revealed knowledge."

"How true. I don't suppose you have any insights to offer on the lighthouse murder?"

"None whatever. There are already too many fools opining on that sordid affair. I hope you will try not to be one of them."

"I don't intend to be," said Max, not sure of where this bizarre conversation might be heading. "Of course, a man may be a fool and not even know it."

The man took a puff on his cigar.

"Not if he has a wife."

Then he turned and left, leaving Max with a bewildered look on his face. Another man working nearby in the clippings room chuckled to himself.

Max turned to the man. "Do you know that guy?"

"Everybody knows that guy. Mister, you just met the Sage of Baltimore; the one and only H.L. Mencken. You might even show up in his next editorial."

"I'm glad it wasn't Hal Marks."

"Hal Marks? You're looking for Hal Marks? That's me."

"A stroke of luck at last. I'm Max Hurlock from over in St Michael's and I'm investigating the lighthouse murder. I've been reading your reports on it. I assume you went to Crisfield?"

"Yep. I was there for three days and I interviewed a bunch of people."

"What was your impression of the case?"

Marks lit a cigarette. "Hard to say. I usually cover crime stories and I've seen plenty of dicey things. People kill each other for lots of reasons, but it always seems to come down to some relative or friend who wanted to settle a score, or maybe figured he'd gain in some way, or maybe just lost his head for a bit. If it isn't that, it's jealousy or some lover's fight. What I'm getting at is that the killer is usually pretty obvious."

"That's not the case at the lighthouse," Max reminded him.

"No, it's not. It's murky and confused. There's all kinds of undercurrents going on. I even met people who swear the Virginia oystermen are responsible. The theory is that the lighthouse keeper was telling the Maryland Oyster Patrol whenever he saw a boat he didn't recognize. Chances are it was a Virginia boat trying to horn in on Maryland oyster beds. Some folks in Crisfield figure the Virginians needed to shut him up for good."

"Did you find anything to support that idea?"

"Not a thing. I suppose it was just a rumor. The Maryland watermen don't have much use for Virginians that come to work Maryland oyster beds. Aside from it being illegal, the Virginians use dredges pulled by power boats. That's illegal even for Marylanders and causes a lot of damage to the beds; rips them up something fierce. It's not unknown for the Maryland men and the Virginia men to brawl or even trade gunfire about it. With all that going on, killing a lighthouse keeper might be considered small change."

"How about Coleman's contacts in Crisfield?"

"I found several people that knew him, but only a few disliked him. There was a guy named Paisley…"

"I know about him. Anyone else?"

"As a matter of fact, Paisley's wife didn't seem to think Jack Coleman was the cat's pajamas either. A few of the waterman grumbled a little about Coleman spying on them and reporting them to either the Oyster Police or the Coast Guard for one thing or another, but I never found anything concrete. It was just talk as far as I could tell."

"Did you talk to the Lighthouse Service?"

"I dropped into their headquarters in D.C. and looked through their reports and records, but there wasn't anything that looked unusual. Jack Coleman had a clean record operations wise, but they don't let you look at personnel records, so who really knows? One thing I picked up; they want this case finished and put to bed. The Lighthouse Service has people scattered all over the country in isolated locations and they don't want the other keepers panicking and shooting anyone who shows up unannounced. I'll let you see my notes if you'd like."

"Thanks. I would like to look them over briefly."

A few minutes later, Max was in Marks's office looking through his notes and finding little he didn't already know. He stood up, placed the notes back in the file and thanked Marks for his help.

"Are you heading back to the Eastern Shore soon, Mr. Hurlock?"

"On the first steamboat tomorrow morning," Max answered. "I learned about all I can here, and I have to get back before two friends of mine turn their life savings over to a con man."

"Well, good luck."

As Max was about to leave, the telephone rang and Marks picked it up.

"Yeah, this is Marks. What? When?" He grabbed a pen and started writing. "Well, can you beat that? All right. Thanks." He hung up the telephone and turned to Max.

"That was one of our stringers over on the shore. It seems there's been another murder at the Devil's Elbow light."

John Reisinger

Chapter 19

The mermaid

Back at the Belvedere, Max and the telephone operator tried to place a call to Sergeant Bentley's office, but the line was busy.

"Another murder," said Max, "and this time I not only don't know the killer, I don't even know who the victim was."

"Have they identified the body?" said Allison.

"I don't even know that. I can't get through to Fred Bentley in Crisfield."

"Maybe it isn't related to the case at all," suggested Allison. "Maybe it's just a coincidence."

Max was still on the phone. "I don't think so. Crisfield isn't the sort of place that has bodies turn up every week. Hey, it's finally ringing."

"About time."

"Fred? It's Max Hurlock. I'm in Baltimore, but I'll be back in St Michaels tomorrow. What happened?"

"It's the damndest thing, Max. One of the watermen was passing by the Devil's Elbow light at low tide and saw something washed up on the Devil's Elbow bar. He got close enough to see it was a body and called me. I got out there with a deputy and the coroner. We figured it could have been thrown from the light and drifted there."

"Yes, but who was it?"

"Oh. Didn't I mention it? I must be getting old. I could have sworn…"

"Fred, who was it?"

"Why, it was Billy Thebold. Someone went and bashed him on the head. The coroner said he looked like he'd only been dead a few hours."

"Fred, are you sure that was Billy Thebold? Sometimes being in the water makes a body look different."

"Oh, it was Billy, clear enough. He even had that mermaid tattoo on his arm."

"M…mermaid tattoo?"

As Allison overheard this exchange, her eyes widened.

"Sure. Didn't you know that? 'Course his sleeve usually covered it, but it was there. Anyway, until somebody can prove it actually happened at the lighthouse, I'm assuming it's my case, or at least the county's. Are you coming down to Crisfield?"

"Yes. Probably tomorrow. Can you meet me with the automobile?"

"Sure, just give me a call. Anything else?"

"Yes. Could you get me the tide and current table for the area?"

"The coroner and I already checked on that, Max. Billy was killed around ten last night. We estimate that the body drifted to the bar from somewhere in the vicinity of the Devil's Elbow light. That place is downright dangerous."

"Any idea what Billy was doing out at the light?"

"Not a hint. The new lighthouse keeper says he never saw Billy or anyone else out there last night, so if he's telling the truth, Billy must have been in a boat when he was killed."

"I assume no boat was found adrift in that area."

"Nope. It wasn't an accident. Billy didn't just hit his head and fall off his own boat. He was murdered sure as shootin'."

That night, Max and Allison were at the Hippodrome Theater in Baltimore to watch Houdini. When they arrived, Max's mind was in turmoil, thinking of all the implications of another murder and itching to get back to the Eastern Shore. Soon, however, even Max got caught up in the spectacle and showmanship of the performance. Here was a true master at work.

Houdini had been starring in movies for several years, but still performed and had lost none of his legendary showmanship. Early in the performance, Max and Allison were delighted to see the brick wall trick Houdini had mentioned.

"Now, I would like to have a committee of audience members come up on stage and surround the area to make sure I do not go over, under, or around the wall. Are the Hurlocks in the audience tonight?"

Allison raised her hand quickly, almost jumping out of her seat.

"Would you and your husband be part of the committee?"

Max and Allison found themselves on the wide stage under the lights with six other audience members. They examined the wall, spaced themselves around the area, and the illusion began. Just as Houdini had said, the wall was solid masonry. There was no door, secret panel or other opening. Underneath was a large carpet, making the use of any trapdoors in the stage impossible. When the curtains were placed, the ends of the wall protruded into the audience's view, so Houdini could not simply walk around it. The curtains were erected by assistants so that the top of the wall was still visible, and the orchestra played suspenseful music. After a few minutes, the assistants reappeared and dropped he curtains.

There was Houdini, casually standing on the other side of the wall. The theater erupted into applause and Houdini bowed, then thanked the committee members. When he got to Max and Allison, he winked and kissed Allison's hand.

The next morning, Max and Allison took the steamboat back to Claiborne. Allison was still excited about the performance and their part in it, but Max couldn't get his mind off of Billy Thebold and wondered why anyone would kill him.

That afternoon, Max took off in Gypsy for Crisfield and Allison wrote more of her article.

> As Houdini has been documenting recently, many if not most mediums are outright frauds. At a recent séance in Baltimore, Houdini showed how they use simple magic tricks to make objects appear and sneaky assistants to produce other "manifestations". They prey on the gullible who want to believe and they charge them a steep price for doing it.
>
> Houdini and others are performing a public service by exposing these tricksters wherever they find them. After all, losing a loved one is bad enough without encountering a medium who will take advantage of your grief to fleece you. The tricks might be phony, and

the contact with the departed might be bogus, but the money the spiritualists will take from their victims is all too real.

She looked at what she had written. "Not bad. But now that I know about her tricks, I think I should talk to Madame DeSousa once again."
She started up the Model T and headed for Easton.

"I'm glad you could come back, Max," said Sergeant Bentley when he picked up Max at the farm outside of town. "This whole place is buzzin' and now I got to get to the bottom of it."
"Is it really in your jurisdiction?"
"The county D.A.'s office called and put me in charge, seein' as how I knew Billy and the town."
"I see. Do you have any theories?" Max asked.
"I got several of 'em, and they all involve Tom Paisley."
"A reasonable hypothesis. Have you talked to him?"
"No, actually. He seems to have disappeared."
"How about Nell?"
"I questioned her this morning. She says she doesn't know where Tom went. Claims he never said anything about goin' anywhere. We're checking on his relatives in case he went to one of them."
"So it's just a case of jealousy and revenge? Then where does the lighthouse keeper fit in to it?"
"The way I figure it," said Sergeant Bentley, "Nell was seein' Jack Coleman and Billy both. Tom knew about Coleman, but he thought Billy was out of the picture since he flattened him at the club that night a while back. But Jack Coleman wasn't so easily discouraged. He kept comin' around and probably Nell was visiting him at the lighthouse as well. Maybe he

even caught them there together that night. That would explain the table set for two we found there."

"Wait a minute," said Max. "If Tom already knew about Nell's affair with Jack Coleman, why would Nell be so anxious to get Coleman's diary after he was dead?"

Bentley frowned. "Maybe the diary said that Billy was still in the picture and she was protectin' him. Or maybe Jack Coleman was blackmailin' Nell, threatening to tell Tom about Billy."

"That would explain Billy's remark about Coleman's blackmail scheme," Max observed.

"Well" said Sergeant Bentley, "I haven't got everything figured out, but I think I got a good start."

Max nodded. "You've been busy, and what you say makes a lot of sense."

"I know that tone of voice, Max. You got doubts. Now what are you thinkin'?"

"I just wonder if we're not making an awful lot of assumptions here. Besides, where does the radio come in?"

"Aw, geez, Max. Not that damned radio again. Well maybe he was using it to contact Nell, or maybe he liked to talk to other lonely lighthouse keepers, or maybe, just maybe, it didn't have anything to do with the murders at all."

"Maybe."

"Anyway, I've taken Nell into custody until I can track down Tom. I have the patrolmen asking around to find him."

"Where is the body now?"

"It's at a funeral home in town. We're trying to find relatives."

"Have your boys been looking around the Paisley Club now that the owners are out of the way?"

"Yeah, we looked around. We found bootleg alcohol and some paperwork concerning buying from local dealers, but nothing beyond that."

"Uh huh. Do you mind if I ask Nell Paisley some questions when we get to your office?"

"Be my guest, but she's not exactly bustin' to tell us anything. Meanwhile the Paisley Club is shut down seein' as how there's nobody left to run it."

As they approached Bentley's office, Max noticed the CG-182 tied up at the steamboat wharf.

"What's the Coast Guard doing here? Don't tell me they're looking into Billy's murder too."

"Naw. The CG-182 is sort of layin' in wait to get the jump on the runners. They do that sometimes. The chief says they heard a rumor that a big shipment is due to go out tonight. They're ready to get after it right quick once it's good and dark."

"Prohibition never sleeps, I guess."

Madame DeSousa had just finished a reading when Allison arrived. The front door opened as Allison approached and the previous client emerged. The client was about Allison's age and looked concerned. She smiled faintly as she passed by. Another victim, Allison thought, as she stepped into the front parlor.

Madame DeSousa closed the front door and the room was suddenly quiet. She was pleased to see Allison again.

"Allison, my dear. How nice to see you. What can I do for you?"

They sat in two overstuffed chairs in the parlor. Madame DeSousa offered tea, but Allison declined.

"Madame DeSousa, I've just returned from Baltimore. I attended a séance with your mentor, Irene Sterling."

"Oh, I see." The medium was suddenly wary. "Was that the séance where..."

"Yes, it was. Houdini made an appearance. It was extremely enlightening. It was sort of a magic show in which Houdini made Irene Sterling's credibility disappear."

Madame DeSousa shook her head sadly. "Wretched man. He's causing so many problems for the spiritual community."

"I imagine he is," said Allison. "You see, he explained the so-called manifestations I saw at your séance. I know about the fishing lines, the gauze ectoplasm, the assistants who wander around, and the heelless shoe you use to free up your foot to work switches."

"But Allison, surely you don't think my spirits are some parlor trick?"

"That's exactly what I think, Madame DeSousa, or should I say Maude Flannagan?"

"But..."

"The only spirit around this house is the spirit of commerce," said Allison. "You are a fraud, just like your mentor, Irene Sterling. You use tricks to convince gullible people and to fool them into thinking they have contact with the afterlife. You give them false hope that they can actually communicate with dead loved ones, but it's all a show."

Madame DeSousa sat with her head bowed for a moment, then answered in a soft voice.

"And is that really so bad?"

Allison was startled by the answer. "What? Of course it is. It's fraud."

Madame DeSousa nodded. "Yes, it is in a way, but let me show you something." She stood up and crossed to a small desk and removed a ledger.

"Here is a list of my clients. It makes for interesting reading."

She pointed to a name. "This lady came to me when her youngest child died of Scarlet Fever last June. She was crushed and was thinking of suicide. Here's another name. This man lost his wife in an accident for which he blamed himself. Her memory tormented him so that he couldn't sleep and hardly ate. He came to me for closure; for release from the terrible burden of guilt. He thought if he could only talk to her once more and explain what had happened it would be all right. Here is a woman who lost her mother to the Spanish Flu when her mother visited New York. The woman was devastated that she never got to say good bye. I could go on, Allison. This book is full of people like that because the world is full of people like that."

She closed the book softly and placed it on a table.

"These are people whose very souls are in torment. They have lost someone very close and have unfinished business that now can never be resolved. And where can they go for relief? To the church? To friends? To other family members? No. No one really understands and no one can give comfort except the departed. Yes, Allison, you are right. I am a fake. I use tricks and psychology to bring comfort to people that are crying out for it. I give them closure so they can live the rest of their lives in peace. I know they are not really in communication with their loved ones, but who would tell them that? Would you have the heart to crush someone's hopes by telling them there is no real way to communicate with the dead? So I ask you once more; is what I do so bad?"

"But you make money off of other people's misery."

"No, Allison. I make money *relieving* other people's misery. Isn't that what a doctor does?"

"A doctor cures people…"

"And so do I. My clients come to me crushed and distraught, and they leave with peace of mind they could get nowhere else. Why do you think Conan Doyle is so determined to believe? It's because he has such a void in his heart from the death of his son that only communication with the son will fill it. So tell me, Allison, which is better; helping him through a harmless deceit, or slamming the door in his face?"

"I understand what you are saying, but what about Mabel Johnson? That woman is poor. She can't afford two dollars for a session, no matter how much good it does her."

Madame DeSousa nodded.

"I agree with you, Allison. That's why I only charge her twenty five cents for each session. In her case, I would do it for free, but I know she's too proud to accept charity. As for the others, the price varies with what they can afford. Yes, I make a good living, but I work for it, and I believe I am performing a service. My clients can always replace the money I charge them, but they can't replace their loved ones who are gone. So yes, Allison, I am a fake, but I like to think I am a fake in a good cause. If you expose me, where will the people in that book go for relief? Who will sooth them in the depths of their grief? Who will help fill the terrible void in their hearts?"

The room was silent for a moment except for the ticking of a clock on the mantle.

"Well, you've given me a new perspective," Allison admitted, "but there's one thing I don't understand. If you're a fake, how did you know about Max having a case and about how he should look out for a mermaid?"

Madame DeSousa looked confused.

"I…I really don't know. Yes, almost everything I do is made up, but once in a while, I really do get a premonition. I can't predict it, and I certainly can't explain it, but I saw a mermaid when I talked to you. Maybe it's the power of suggestion, spending so much time talking about the supernatural, or maybe sometimes, somehow, I really do get a little glimpse behind the curtain. I just don't know. It frightens me sometimes. Why do you ask?"

"Because they just had a murder down in Crisfield and the victim had a tattoo of a mermaid on his arm."

"Oh, dear."

The jail in the back of the Crisfield Police station had only two cells and a drunk was sleeping it off in one of them. Nell Paisley was in the other cell, looking small as she huddled moodily on the cot.

"You have a visitor, Nell," said Bentley.

She looked up. "Oh, it's you again. Mr. Hurlock, right?"

Max smiled. "That's right. I'd like to talk to you if you don't mind."

She looked around the cell. "Well, I'm not too busy at the moment, as you can see."

"I'll leave you two to chat," said Bentley. "I think it's time to empty the other cell anyway. He's had time to sleep it off. Seems like the more illegal liquor gets the more drunks I gotta entertain."

Max pulled up a metal chair just outside the bars.

"Nell, what do you know about Billy Thebold?"

"Aside from the fact that Tom killed him you mean?"

"Did he? How do you know?"

"Well, I don't know for sure, but Tom had no use for Billy and I figure he found out we were still seeing each other. Like I told you, Tom's got a bad temper. I always knew that, but he's gone too far this time."

"So you think Tom killed Billy because he found out Billy was still seeing you?"

She shrugged. "Nobody else would have any reason to want Billy dead."

Max sat casually in the chair and talked in a conversational manner. "So what kind of guy was Billy?"

"Oh, he was real nice, but a little private."

"Private?"

"He was a bookkeeper, but he talked about other things he was doing to make more money. Then he'd never say exactly what they were. Something to do with radios, I think."

"So where did he work?"

"He was working some part time jobs up around Salisbury. He did book keeping for some of the farmers around there, especially Arthur Perdue."

"I know him," said Max. "He's in the egg business."

Nell nodded. "Right. He has a lot of customers in different places to keep track of, so he needed a part time bookkeeper once in a while, but that's a family run business. Arthur and his wife Pearl took care of most of the paperwork and they had a son Franklin who would be helping out when he got older, so there wasn't any full time work for a bookkeeper. Billy told him he could really expand his egg business if he borrowed some money from the bank, maybe build a hatchery, but Mr. Perdue didn't want to go into debt, so he expanded too slow to take Billy on full time."

"So Billy did something with a radio?"

"Yeah. Once or twice he let slip that he was doing some work as a radio operator somewhere. That was about all he ever said about it, though."

"What was the last thing Billy said to you before he disappeared?"

"Uh, let's see. He said he was meeting somebody on a business deal."

"Did he say who?"

"No, he never told me who he was meeting, but I think he said he was going out on a boat somewhere."

John Reisinger

Chapter 20

The fugitive

All the way back to St Michaels, Allison's head was spinning. Suddenly, she had a new perspective on spiritualism and spiritualists. Well, some of them, anyway. Sometimes, it seemed, deception could be employed in a good cause.

But usually it was not.

Allison stopped by the St Michaels Post Office to pick up the mail. As she strolled out on the dusty street shuffling through several letters, she saw Thelma Lonnigan, the switchboard operator making her way across the street with a basket of groceries.

"Afternoon, Allison."

"Hello, Thelma. Who's minding the St Michaels switchboard?"

"Lands sakes, child. I don't live at that switchboard. I get relieved now and again. I got to get home with these groceries and get Elmer his dinner. Lord, I believe that man would starve to death if it wasn't for me. One time he got impatient and tried to fry an egg on his own. It took a week to air out the kitchen. Anyway, that's why I'm getting home. I'm not taking any chances that he'll try a durned fool thing like that again."

Allison laughed uneasily. Her cooking efforts had not always met with complete success either.

"You know that Martha Hess over on Thompson Street has been talking to that Will Davis several times a day. If you ask me there's something going on there, but I'm not one to carry gossip," said Thelma.

"I can see that."

"You didn't hear it from me, Allison."

"My ears are sealed. Well, I have to be getting home, Thelma. Good luck with Elmer's dinner."

"Oh, I'll be fine. I got extra scrapple today. Elmer does love his scrapple."

"Yes, it's one of the finest of the gray meats," said Allison, slowly backing away. "Well, bon appetite."

Thelma started away, then turned back suddenly.

"Oh, Allison. I almost forgot. Someone called for Max earlier today."

"Max went to Crisfield, and I've been up in Easton."

Thelma started fumbling in her purse. "I made a note at the time. Now where did I put it? Here it is...no. that's my grocery list. Oh, here it is."

She handed Allison a crumbled up piece of paper.

"Thanks" said Allison, placing the paper in her purse. "I'll see that Max gets it."

The Model T chugged softly as Allison turned into the driveway to the house. She always loved the way the house slowly came into view through the trees as she got closer.

"I'll check in with Max in Crisfield, then have a little peace and quiet to work on my article," she said out loud. "I'll just kick off these shoes and…oh, no."

J.D. and Casper were waiting on the porch.

They stood up with their hats in their hands as Allison rolled to a stop by the front steps.

"Hiya fellas. How's tricks?"

"Hello Miz Allison. We called here a bunch of times. We're trying to get ahold of Max."

"He's in Crisfield. I'm just about to call him. Hold on a second."

In a minute, she had placed a call to Sergeant Bentley's office in Crisfield. There was no answer.

"Well, he's down there, but I guess he's out somewhere with Fred Bentley. I'll just have to try again later."

"That's all right. We're heading down that way anyhow, so we'll catch up with him there. You see, we finally raised the money for Gaston Means and we promised Max we'd tell him before we turned it over. Tomorrow's the deadline, so we got no choice. Max tried his best for us, but I guess even Max can't work miracles. We appreciate him tryin' though. We'll be headin' out in the Karen Rebecca. Afternoon, Miz Allison."

"Wait a minute" said Allison. "Hop in the flivver. The least I can do is give you a lift."

A few minutes later, they were standing by the dock at Claiborne. J.D. and Casper climbed into the Karen Rebecca and began to untie the lines. Allison suddenly remembered the note from Thelma Lonnigan.

"Say, fellas, when you find Max, could you give him a note?"

She took a quick glance at the note. "Wait a minute. Do you fellas have room in the boat for one more? I think I'd better give this to Max myself."

"Well, that just about settles it," said Sergeant Bentley. "If Tom Paisley didn't kill Jack Coleman and Billy Thebold, then grits ain't groceries. Why, Nell practically confessed for him."

Sergeant Bentley and Max were heading north toward Deal. One of the deputies said Tom Paisley's brother lived there. Sergeant Bentley always said that a fugitive will always head for home first.

"I admit it looks bad for Tom Paisley, and his actions fit in pretty well," said Max. "We'll just have to find him and have a little talk. There has to be more to the story."

"Sure there is," said Bentley, "and it's not hard to figure out. Old Tom found out about Jack Coleman and went out to that light. I talked to some people who told me he wasn't around the Paisley Club the night Jack was killed. It all fits together. Then he found out about Billy Thebold still hangin' around about the time you did, so he figured he might as well take care of him as well. I figure he took Billy out to the light to kill him to make it look like Billy was killed by maybe rumrunners or Virginia oystermen."

"Very neat," said Max, "assuming that's what happened, of course. Maybe we'll find out more from Tom Paisley himself."

Tom Paisley's brother Hal was a waterman with a shack near Haines Point on Deal Island. Max and Sergeant Bentley found the shack in a cluster of several similar ones. The houses faced a creek and there were several piers with workboats tied up and stacks of rope, tongs and crab traps everywhere. Max and Sergeant

Bentley walked up to the house slowly. A woman wearing a faded brown dress and a headscarf answered the door.

"Hal's out on the water," she said. "He'll be back around seven or eight; maybe sooner if he finds a buy boat and doesn't have to stop at the cannery."

"Yes, Ma'am," said Bentley. "Has his brother Tom been around recently?"

"Can't say."

Sergeant Bentley squinted at her sharply. "Does that mean you don't know or that the answer's yes but you're not tellin'?"

"I got things to do."

She slammed the door.

"Well, she didn't want to tell you much, Fred," said Max as they walked away.

Sergeant Bentley smiled. "She didn't want to, but she told me plenty. Tom Paisley's been there. He might even be there now. I'll get one of my boys to stake out the house."

"I wouldn't bother with that," said Max, looking over Sergeant Bentley's shoulder. "I think you'll find Tom Paisley in the third house to the left."

Bentley spun his head around. "What? The third house on the left? Why do you say that?"

"Because I just saw Mrs. Paisley dash over there and I don't think it was to borrow a cup of sugar."

"Dang! And I never got me an arrest warrant."

"You don't need to arrest him, at least not yet. You just need to have a little talk with him and see what's what. You can arrest him later if you need to."

"I'll give it a try. No offense. Max, but I wish I'd a brought a cop instead of you."

Max smiled. "So do I, but you talk calmly to old Tom and maybe he'll respond."

"Yeah. Maybe."

Sergeant Bentley and Max went back down the common driveway of the shacks and up to the one Max had spotted Mrs. Paisley running to.

"Hey, Tom. This here's Fred Bentley. Why don't we have us a little talk?"

The house was silent.

"Try it again," said Max.

"Now, Tom, I know you're in there. I ain't got a patrolman with me, but if you don't talk to me I'll have to bring a couple. Right now, though, I just want to talk."

There was still no answer.

"Tom, you know I got to question you, but I don't have to arrest you, not if you can convince me you didn't kill Billy Thebold. Now we had us some run ins from time to time, but you got to allow as how I always treated you squarely, and that's what I intend to do now."

The door began to open.

"Good going, Fred," said Max.

But Mrs. Paisley appeared.

"He ain't coming, Sergeant. He won't be hanged on account of that Billy Thebold. He's got to lay low until the truth comes out. Now you just get on back to Crisfield and do whatever you got to do. Tom ain't comin' back with you. He knows you'd treat him fairly, but he can't take the chance with a jury."

"Well, I think I'll just give it another…"

Sergeant Bentley stopped. From behind the houses came the sound of a boat starting up.

"I'll be a …"

Bentley and Max ran around the side of the house just in time to see a small work boat pull away, driven by Tom Paisley. Bentley threw his hat on the ground.

"Son of a...What are you smiling about, Max?"

Max stifled a smile. "Sorry, Fred, but it just occurred to me that we've been the victims of a smooth piece of misdirection, courtesy of Mrs. Paisley here."

"I'm sure I don't know what you're talking about," sniffed Mrs. Paisley.

"Oh, I think you do," said Max, "but never mind. We have to be getting back to Crisfield to find a boat."

They were back in the automobile and down the road to Crisfield in a few seconds.

"Dang it, Max, by the time we get hold of a boat, he could be anywhere. All he's got to do is cross the creek and disappear into the woods."

Max said nothing. He sat frowning.

"Fred, Mrs. Paisley said he had to lie low until the truth came out. What do you suppose that meant?"

"Not a danged thing," Sergeant Bentley grumbled. "They always say things like that when they're trying to wriggle out of something. Seems to me the truth is already out; he just don't like it."

But Max didn't answer.

The Karen Rebecca was off of Taylor's Island and helped along by a brisk north wind, chugged south as fast as she could go, rising and falling gently with the swell. As waves slapped the bow, throwing up gouts of spray, Casper steered and J.D. fussed and made adjustments to the engine. Allison sat huddled near the bow, as if she wanted to be the first to arrive. Several times during the passage, she took out the crumpled paper in her pocket, looked at it, then put it back.

Back in Crisfield, Fred Bentley rounded up two boats with police to comb the creeks around Deal to find Tom Paisley. Then he put in a call to the Somerset

County Sheriff's Office in Princess Anne for more men to help with the search. Max decided to split up with Sergeant Bentley and do some investigating on his own, but just as he was starting towards the door, Brian Murphy arrived and asked to see Sergeant Bentley.

"Afternoon, Brian," said Bentley. "This is a rare treat, I have to say. I don't believe I've ever seen you in this office."

Murphy looked uneasy.

"Can we talk in private?"

"Sure. Close the door. I assume you don't mind if Max listens in?"

"No. That's fine. Look, you know I've been rumored to be mixed up with rumrunning from time to time."

Sergeant Bentley shrugged. "Well, you know how rumors spread."

Murphy sat down, twisting his hat in his hands.

"Now I'm not saying there's any truth to the rumors, mind you, but there's something you need to know."

"I'm all ears, Brian."

Murphy looked around.

"Look, you know I'm not a stool pigeon. I never rat on anybody, but…"

"But what?"

"I think I can help you find Tom Paisley."

"Can you, now? But why would you want to do that? What have you got against Tom?"

"I don't have a thing against Tom, Fred, and I have no idea if he's guilty or not, but I figure it this way; you're going to catch him sooner or later anyway, but while you're looking for him, this town and all the waterways around it will be crawling with deputies. Now it makes no difference to me you understand, but I do have a lot of friends around here and, well, some of them run 'shine once in a while."

"Do tell," said Sergeant Bentley.

"The thing is, I don't want any of them getting in trouble just because they run into one of those extra deputies. So I figure if I help you find Tom, the extra deputies won't be needed and it'll make the area safer for my friends."

Sergeant Bentley turned to Max.

"Now there's a real humanitarian for you, Max."

Max didn't respond.

"Well, Brian," said Bentley, turning to Murphy, "I'm a suspicious guy. Comes with the job, I guess. I can't help thinking that this concern for protecting rumrunners is a little closer to home than you're letting on."

Murphy started to protest, but Sergeant Bentley held up his hand.

"However, I do need to find Tom Paisley, so your motives, whatever they are, don't concern me. Now, where is he?"

"I don't know for sure, but a couple of my pals just called me and said they saw him in a boat heading towards Bloodsworth Island. They figure he's going over there to lay low for a while."

Sergeant Bentley nodded.

"Not a bad choice. It's big, isolated and it's surrounded by shallow water. Just the sort of place if you don't want company, so long as you take plenty of provisions with you. All right, Brian, we'll send some boys over there to check it out."

"You won't tell anyone I tipped you off?"

"I won't breathe a word."

Brian Murphy stood up and backed away.

"Thanks, Fred. Thanks to you both."

When Murphy was gone, Bentley shook his head.

"His friends? His clients more likely. I can see through him like a broken window. He's clearing the way for his rumrunning pals, getting' the police searching north while his boys go south. Still, if it gets me Tom Paisley, I don't mind a bit. I'll take few men up there, just in case he's tellin' the truth. I just have to make a few phone calls."

"Good luck, Fred," said Max. "I guess you don't need me anymore. I'm going to go and have a look around on my own. I'll probably check along the waterfront to see if anyone's seen anything."

Max left Sergeant Bentley and wandered off. He went along the dock areas talking to people, then up to the Paisley Club, but it was locked and empty. Finally, he decided to drop in on Gaston Means.

Means was sitting on the front porch of the Commercial Hotel like a spider waiting for a fly. Once again, he was dressed in a dark blue suit with a vest and a bow tie. He put down the paper he was reading when he saw Max.

"Ah, good evening Mr. Hurlock."

"Mr. Means. Have you made any progress with your investigation?"

Means smiled. "Why, yes. I have obtained copies of reports from both the Lighthouse Service and the Coast Guard. I also have statements from several of the people around here. They're in my briefcase here. You may look at them if you'd like."

"I would like that."

Means handed Max the briefcase and Max thumbed through a ream of reports and ledger sheets. It was pretty routine stuff for the most part, just the sort of thing one government agency would send to another, but it gave the impression of a thorough investigation.

He even saw copies of the Coast Guard report he had seen in Baltimore. Means was at least making a show of investigating.

"And I suppose your mysterious Mr. Smith has still refused to meet anyone but you?"

"Alas, yes."

Max was still looking through the papers as he spoke. "You know, Mr. Means, I'm a suspicious guy. When I see something that doesn't add up, I start to ask why. And as far as I can see, your story about Mr. Smith doesn't add up at all."

"I can't help that. Sometimes the truth is hard to believe. You should take that up with Mr. Smith. He's the one who made the proposition."

"I have a proposition of my own, Mr. Means."

Means looked wary. "Oh? What would that be?"

"It's very simple. If my friends show up with money in hand, you refuse to take it, and you do not file charges against them."

Means leaned back and tented his fingers over his ample stomach.

"I see. And what do I get in return, Mr. Hurlock?"

Max looked up from the papers. "In return, I don't tell Hal Marks from the Baltimore Sun about how you're trying to squeeze honest working men out of their life savings."

"You know Mr. Marks personally?"

"I spoke to him just a few days ago about the case. He's been assigned to cover it you know. I promised to let him know about anything I turned up that might be newsworthy. I think this story qualifies."

"I'll deny it."

"I have three witnesses that heard your claims. But what will really be interesting will be what happens when you have to produce Mr. Smith. Marks is a good reporter. He knows how to dig, but he doesn't know how to give up. Once he gets his teeth on a bone like this, he won't stop until everything comes out in the open for the world to see. I'm only telling you this as one investigator to another. I'd hate to see you embarrassed nedlessly."

Means was silent for a moment. Max went back to going through the papers. Finally, Means spoke in a noncommittal tone.

"I...I will take this under advisement."

Max stopped and pulled out a paper.

"Mr. Means, I assume you visited the lighthouse and looked around?"

"The lighthouse? Yes, of course. Why do you ask?"

"I assume you noticed a new two way radio and aerial had been installed?"

"I do seem to recall a radio of some kind. Why?"

"This is a list of invoices paid by the Lighthouse Service for the Devil's Elbow light for the past year. There is no mention of a new radio or aerial."

"So what?"

"So the lighthouse keeper must have installed the radio, or at least the aerial on his own. Now why would he do that?"

Means shook his head. "I assume you are alluding to the rumor that Mr. Coleman was killed by rumrunners because he was using his radio to inform the Coast Guard of their movements. As a matter of fact I did look into that allegation and found there is nothing to it. You have the Coast Guard reports right there. If they were informed by radio of any such activity, they would have recorded it. Their reports are quite thorough and make no mention of being informed by Mr. Coleman of anything. No, Mr. Hurlock, that is one part of this case that is no mystery; Jack Coleman was <u>not</u> using that radio to inform the Coast Guard."

Max thought about it a moment, then stood up to leave.

"You know, I believe you are right about that. Good evening, Mr. Means."

John Reisinger

Chapter 21

The boat house

The Karen Rebecca reached the steamship dock in Crisfield a little after six and tied up next to the CG-182. The shadows were long but it wasn't dark yet. As J.D. and Casper were securing the boat, Allison bounded out and across the railroad tracks.

Allison made her way across Main Street along the sidewalk next to the rails and across the street from the packing houses and commercial buildings to Sergeant Bentley's office. When she got there, she almost collided with Sergeant Bentley as he was starting up his automobile.

"Well, evening, Allison. I didn't know you were down here."

"Where's Max?"

"Max? Oh, he said he was going to walk along the waterfront and see what he could find out. I expect he'll be back soon."

"I have to see him right away."

"Well, I have to join a couple of my boys on a manhunt for Tom Paisley while we still have some light. I'm sorry, but I can't look for Max right now. I have to get going. I'll see you later."

Then with a roar and a grinding of gears, he was pulling away before Allison had a chance to tell him why she needed to see Max.

"Fred, wait!"

But he was already too far away to hear.

"Rats. All right. I'll find him myself."

Allison rushed into the office and wrote a note for Max in case she missed him, then set out along the Crisfield waterfront as the light was fading.

Max stopped in at the pool hall on his way back to Sergeant Bentley's office and talked to a few of the men there. No one seemed in the least surprised that Tom Paisley was now a fugitive on a murder charge. The only surprise seemed to be that something like that hadn't happened sooner.

"Hell, it was only a matter of time afor somethin' like this happened," one of them said. "Those two were always runnin' around on each other and fightin' like two bobcats in a box about it. 'Couse, I always thought one of them would kill the other, not someone else."

"Yeah," said another. "Ol' Billy used to brag that he got Tom's goat. Looks like that goat done butted Billy good."

"Any idea where Tom Paisley might go to get away?"

"He got a brother over in Deal and I think a cousin on Smith Island, but that's all I ever heard."

Another man shook his head in disbelief.

"Tom always said he'd settle things with Jack Coleman, but everybody thought it was just talk. I guess you just never know."

Allison was impatient and increasingly frustrated. She had been up and down the waterfront streets and there was no sign of Max. The light was fading and she was now as far away from the police station as she dared to go, an area of broken down buildings, cold looking packing plants, piles of oyster shells, and ramshackle boathouses on the edge of the industrial area. Her feet were hurting and she was ready to give up, go back, and resign herself to waiting.

"Drat. I'll never find him at this rate, and it'll be dark soon anyway. Maybe he's back at Sergeant Bentley's office by now."

At that moment, Max was at Dr. Ward's Drug store just a few blocks away, where he had stopped after leaving the pool hall. He figured Fred Bentley might be gone a while, so he stopped for a sarsaparilla phosphate to collect his thoughts. He sat at the counter of the soda fountain while they mixed his phosphate and he tried to piece together his theory of who killed the lighthouse keeper and Billy Thebold and why. He had a pretty good idea of how everything fit together, but he needed something more; some piece of evidence to act as the glue that made everything stick. But where could he get it? The only problem was figuring out the meaning of the new radio antenna he had seen at the lighthouse. Maybe Fred Bentley was right. Maybe it was a coincidence that meant nothing.

"Here's your phosphate, mister. That'll be twelve cents."

Max fished the money out of his pocket and paid, then sipped his drink moodily.

Thinking about the case and staring into his glass, Max didn't notice J.D. and Casper passing by on the sidewalk outside. He was too preoccupied for anything like that. Besides, he knew J.D. and Casper were back home in Tilghman, just as Allison was back home in St Michaels.

He finished his drink and asked if he could use the telephone. He tried to place a call to Allison, but no one answered.

"Now where could she have gotten to?"

"Well, J.D. here we are."

"Yep. Here we are, No Whiskey."

J.D. and Casper stood across the street from the Hotel Commercial where Gaston Means was staying. They stood under a street light that was just coming on, hesitant to take the final steps that would lead to poverty. J.D. kept fingering the wad of hundred dollar bills in his pocket.

"Lord, I do hate givin' money to that man," said Casper.

"I hate givin' it to anybody. I worked too long and hard for it," said J.D..

"Of course, if he's tellin' the truth, this could crack the case wide open and put us in the clear."

"Not only that, but I read where the Lighthouse Service is offerin' a $5000 reward for anybody who provides information leading to the arrest and conviction of whoever killed their boy. Maybe we could make the money back."

Casper sighed. "Naw. You can bet that Gaston Means would claim he solved the case by turnin' up Mr. Smith. No. J.D., once we turn this money over to Means, it'll be gone forever one way or another."

"A damned shame. You know, you and me been workin' on the water since high school, over ten years now. It's been hard, but we were just startin' to get ahead, just startin' to have some money laid by to build on."

"I was thinkin' of getting' the Karen Rebecca fixed up some, and maybe add a room to the house. Now I don't know if I'll even have a house what with the loan I took out on it. Damn. I really thought old Max would be able to save us in time."

"Even Max can't work miracles, J.D."

"Well, shoot. No point standing here bellyachin'. As long as there's arsters in the bay we'll make that money all over again in the next few years so let's just give it to Mr. Means and hope for the best."

They walked across to the hotel. Once again, Gaston Means was waiting on the front porch.

Allison was making her way back down the street alongside the tracks, to try to get back to Bentley's office before dark. She nervously glanced at several ominous-looking rusty boxcars waiting to be loaded the next day, and shivered as a mangy cat slinked along below one of the cars.

She was just about to pass a side street when she was startled to see a truck come out and turn up Main Street. It was coming out of the driveway to what looked like a shabby boathouse nestled among the much bigger packing houses and surrounded by trees, weeds, and several mounds of oyster shells a half block off of Main Street. What really seemed unusual, however was that the lettering on the side of the truck said "Furniture". Allison stood looking at it with her hands on her hips.

"Who gets a truckload of furniture delivered to a boathouse?" she said aloud. As she said this, an identical truck passed her and stopped before backing down the same driveway.

"Two truckloads of furniture delivered to a broken down boathouse at night? I smell a rat."

She hesitated. Maybe she should just go back and tell Max and Sergeant Bentley about this, but she couldn't be sure of finding either one of them. In addition, it was getting dark and she really wasn't sure what, if anything , was going on in that boathouse.

"Well, I don't suppose it would hurt to have a little peek," she said, and slipped into the woods. Her new shoes immediately protested by rubbing her already sore feet as she made her way over the uneven ground.

As she made her way closer to the boathouse, she could hear muffled voices and the sounds of the truck being unloaded. There were wooden thumping sounds as well, like something was being loaded onto a boat.

She crept closer until she could see in the window. There in the dim light, two men were unloading the back of the truck and carefully stowing crates into a boat. Unlike the shed, the boat was sleek and in good condition. Allison also noted it was painted gray, a hard color to see at night on the water. The boat looked to be at least fifty feet long and bobbed easily in the water. She couldn't see what was in the cases, but from the occasional clinking noises, it was pretty clear it was glassware...or bottles.

This was clearly the beginning of a rumrunning mission, and from what Allison could see, it must be one of the biggest ones ever. With so much at stake, maybe these men were somehow mixed up in the whole business of the lighthouse murders. Max really needed to know about this. She got out a piece of paper and a pencil and wrote down the license number of the truck. Satisfied she had done all she could, she started to turn back toward Sergeant Bentley's office.

Then, a door in the side of the shed opened and a man came out and looked around. Allison quickly squatted down behind a pile of oyster shells. The fishy smell filled her nostrils.

"I'm telling you I heard something out here," the man said.

A voice came from inside. "Forget it, Brian. We're just about ready to head out. It's almost dark."

"I'm sure I heard something moving around out here."

"Probably a cat or something. Anyway, who cares? We'll be gone in a few minutes anyway. Then any nosy parkers can snoop to their heart's content."

A few more seconds passed as the man remained standing in the doorway and Allison held her breath.

"Yeah, I guess you're right, Patrick. I'm just jumpy tonight."

Allison heard the door close and allowed herself to exhale.

"As jumpy as they are, I'd better not move until they're gone," she muttered. "I guess I'm stuck here. Now what's a nice Goucher girl doing sneaking around in the woods and packing plants at night spying on bootleggers?"

"Hey Fred! Anybody home?"

Max looked back and forth as he entered Sergeant Bentley's office, but it was empty. He wasn't really surprised. He expected Fred Bentley and some of the police would be converging on Bloodsworth Island to the north by now. It was probably a diversion but they would check it out anyway.

He looked out the window. It was now dark; too dark to find a man hiding in wetlands. Well, tomorrow would be another day. He sat back in a chair in front of the desk reviewing the details of this confusing case. Could it all come down to Tom Paisley? But what about the radio? The nagging question just wouldn't go away. Why would a man who's <u>not</u> informing the authorities about the rumrunners need a powerful radio?

Max sat up. "Of course. That's why he needed the radio. That's the only possible reason. But then that would mean…yes; that had to be it."

Max stood up and paced the floor working out the details. Now he knew why the lighthouse keeper needed a powerful radio and what he was doing with it, but then how did that fit into the murders?

Maybe once Tom Paisley was captured and questioned, the pieces would all fit together. Maybe he'd have some piece of information that would unlock the rest of the story.

He walked over to the front window. To the left, beyond the end of the nearby boxcar, lights were appearing on the CG-182 and figures moved about the decks making preparations for the night's patrol. He went behind the desk and sat in Fred Bentley's chair to write him a note. He fumbled around the desk to find some paper to write on and suddenly saw the note from Allison.

"Allison? She's up in St Michaels. What in the world?"

He read the note.

> Max:
> I came down here with J.D. and Casper to find you because I can't reach anyone on the telephone. You got a call from Pat Dolan in Cambridge today and he had this message;
>
> "Checked my sales records as promised. The only person I sold a knife to that matches any of the names you gave me is Brian Murphy."

> *Anyway, when I got here, someone said you were on the waterfront, so I'm going to take a walk there and look for you. If you get back before I do, sit tight.*
> *A.*

Brian Murphy. Of course. Now it all made sense. Now he had a pretty good idea of why two people had been murdered. Now it was just a matter of proving it and Max thought he knew just how to do it.

But first he had to find Allison. What in the world was she doing out in the dark? And where is she?

"What are they doing in there?" Allison mumbled. "Let's speed it up, you mugs. I'm getting cold out here."

A sudden rumble from inside the boathouse told her the boat engine had started. The lights in the boathouse went out and were replaced by the smaller running lights of a boat as it pulled slowly out into the harbor. Allison was close enough to see boxes and crates stowed tightly on deck. A large delivery was in progress.

The boat turned and headed towards the harbor entrance. Allison waited until it was out of sight before she dared to move.

"I've got to tell Max about this."

Max looked out of the window onto Main Street. A few people passed by, but where was Allison? She should have been back by now. He'd go after her, but was afraid they'd miss each other in the dark and unfamiliar streets.

Another ten minutes passed. Max couldn't stand pacing the office any longer.

"I guess I'll have to go after her," Max said. "Where could she have gotten to in the dark?"

Max stood in the doorway and looked up and down the street. He didn't even know which way she'd gone.

He went back in the office and found a pair of binoculars and scanned up and down the street. He saw no one.

As he stood in the doorway getting increasingly frustrated, he thought he heard something. He listened again. From up the street, he heard the clicking of a woman's footsteps.

"Hey Max!"

"Allison!"

A few minutes later she was in the office telling Max of her adventure.

"The one guy's name was Brian and the other's name was Patrick," she said breathlessly.

"Then it's the Murphys for sure. What did the boat look like?"

"Maybe 40-50 feet long; low lying with a small cabin near the bow, a big searchlight, and it was packed to the gills with crates of liquor. It's a light gray color with no other markings I could see."

"Did you see these men when you looked in the window?"

"Yes. They looked like brothers, they had..."

"Never mind that. What were they wearing?"

"Wearing?"

"Yes. What were they wearing?"

"Uh, dark blue sweaters, dark pants, dark knit caps, and rubber boots, why?"

"Listen, Allison. You've done a great job, but I have to alert the Coast Guard and go with them. You need to stay here. All right?"

"Don't worry. You won't get me back out there tonight, but why do you have to go? Isn't that up to Fred Bentley and the Coast Guard?"

Death at the Lighthouse

"I have to. Murphy has an important piece of evidence with him he doesn't usually have. I have to take advantage of it or Fred may not be able to prove anything."

"All right, Max. Shove off"

"Good girl. I love you."

Max saw the CG-182 was still there, but was getting ready to cast off. He ran to the gangway.

"I need to see the chief. It's an emergency!"

"We're leaving on patrol, sir."

Chief's Voshel's head appeared on the bridge.

"What's going on?"

"Chief, it's Max Hurlock. I have to talk to you about the patrol."

"I'm listening."

Max explained the situation and how the rumrunner had almost a half hour start.

"I think we can try to run them down, Mr. Hurlock."

"I need to come with you."

"We can't take civilians."

"I understand, chief, but I believe one of those men is a murderer and I need to be there to find the evidence to convict him."

"Wellll..."

"And I think I have a pretty good idea how to catch the disappearing runner."

"Well, why didn't you say so? Climb aboard."

"Thanks, chief."

"Cast off! Helmsman, take us out by way of Kedges Strait and Devil's Elbow light. Half speed ahead until we make the right turn at the harbor entrance channel, then it's full speed all the way."

"Are there any more patrol vessels you could alert?" Max asked.

"There are two smaller ones in the area. I'll send an alert on the radio. Maybe we can get a couple of others as well."

"What are our chances?" Max asked.

"I won't lie to you, Max. Finding a small boat that doesn't want to be found is a tough job, especially at night. These Coast Guard six-bitters will only do fifteen knots or so, and some of the runners do twenty and up."

"Then if the runner has a half-hour head start, we'll never catch her unless she slows down?"

"Not on a straight run, but runners usually twist and turn to evade being tracked. That slows them down. And if another cutter runs into them, that could slow them as well. In addition the weather reports call for a three of four foot chop in the bay tonight. The CG-182 handles rough water a lot better than most runners. So there are a lot of things that could trip them up. We'll just have to keep our fingers crossed."

As the CG-182 moved towards the harbor entrance channel, the row of buildings, boathouses and shacks it passed looked like ragged specters lined up along the water and warning them of dangers ahead. Max looked out over the bow and into the darkness, urging the CG-182 forward.

Chapter 22

The chase

Out in the blackness of the Chesapeake Bay, another small Coast Guard patrol boat bobbed in the swells. The crew scanned the water with binoculars and listened for the sound of boat engines. Suddenly the radio crackled to life.

"This is the CG-182 near Crisfield. All units be on the alert for a runner heading out from the vicinity of Devil's Elbow light. Runner passed the light about fifteen minutes ago and is about 40 to 50 foot in length. No information on its heading."

"If they're heading north they'll be coming our way in a few minutes," said a man looking at the chart.

"Then let's keep our eyes and ears open. It's been a slow night so far. It'd be nice to bag us a runner before we head back."

"Of course, if they're heading for the Potomac, we'll never see her."

After the runner was well past the Devil's Elbow light it had switched off all running lights and turned northwest, a moving dark shape in a world of blackness.

"The water's kicking up some, but it's not too bad. Just try not to let any waves break over us. We're riding kind of low what with all the weight."

"We're doing fine. Don't worry."

"No sign of anyone else out here. Looks like it'll be a smooth operation tonight."

"Maybe, but it's early yet and we've got a long ways to go."

On the Coast Guard patrol boat, they still floated silently, but heard no other sounds.

"I guess that runner went on some other heading. Dang. I was all ready for a good chase, too."

"Yeah, I guess it's time to crank her up and move off to another station and try again. This is as bad as fishing. You wait for a bite and the fish are all somewhere else."

"Well, I guess...Wait a minute."

"What's the matter?"

"I think I hear something."

"Yes. I hear it, too."

He grabbed the binoculars.

"There. Bearing 045."

"I see her. Start the engine. Man the searchlight. Let's get a little closer..."

"Do you think there was really somebody outside when we were loading the goods tonight?"

"I thought so, but I never saw anyone. It doesn't matter now. Even if they reported us, we're long gone."

He looked at his pocket watch in the dim light from the compass.

"We should be past Bloodsworth and closing in on the Choptank soon."

"Hold on."

"You hear something?"

"I think so...and it's getting louder."

"Get ready. I think the Coast Guard is following us."

"I hear them now. Off the port quarter. I'll take the wheel. You get ready, but hold off. Maybe they'll miss us and go right by."

A floodlight washed over the deck of the runner.

"Let's get out of here!"

In a few seconds, the boat slammed into its own wake, tossing violently, and then straightened out.

The light was gone.

On the CG-182, they were following the encounter closely.

"We lost her," came the voice on the radio. "Just like before. One minute it was there, then there was a flash of light and it was gone."

"What course was she following when you approached?" said the chief on the CG-182.

"About 340 degrees, but we've been following that course full speed after she disappeared and there's no sign of her. She just vanished."

"Aye aye."

Max and the chief looked at the chart on the navigation table.

"Here is her last reported position, where the patrol boat lost her. If the disappearing runner was on course 340, it was probably heading for this buoy on a course parallel but outside of the shipping channel, and that means the destination is up the bay somewhere, probably Baltimore or Annapolis. That should give us more time, but a bigger area to search," said the chief.

"Then she probably resumed that course as soon as she shook the other cutter," said Max, examining the chart. Could you plot a course to intercept?"

"If she's doing 20 knots, we'll have a hard time catching her if we can only do 15 or so," said the chief.

"Don't worry, chief. I doubt that runner can do much more than 15 knots, maybe less with a full load."

"How do you know that?"

"It stands to reason. If they could do 20 or 25 knots, why would they have come up with that disappearing trick? All they'd have to do is outrun anyone who got too close, especially at night. No, I think the reason they disappear is because they're slow. We can catch them."

"I hope you're right, Max. Now I'm sure their encounter with the other patrol boat slowed them down, and maybe the rough water will knock her speed down some more. These six-bitters are made for offshore operations so waves won't slow us down as much as a smaller shallow draft rumrunner. We might have a chance to catch up pretty quickly."

Max felt the deck vibrate as the engines rumbled below his feet and the bow split the oncoming waves.

On the rumrunner, confidence was strong.

"That was great. We sure put a knot in his rope," one of the men said.

"Yeah, they went from chasing us to chasing their tail. Those boys are still wondering where we got to."

"We'll give it another five minutes or so, then get back on course 337, but be on the lookout. There might be more around. I'll go check on our cargo. Make sure nothing shook loose in all the excitement."

The motion of the boat was getting more pronounced as the engine surged against the swells.

"You better slow her down a little before she pounds herself to death in these waves."

"All right."

"Good. That's better. We wouldn't want to break any bottles."

The gray hull of the CG-182 sliced through the waves throwing up white spray as it pushed northward at 15 knots. Max went out beside the pilot house and peered into the darkness ahead. The chief came out and stood by him.

"We should be getting close by now," said the chief. I have lookouts posted."

"Great. Maybe we'll both have a successful night."

The chief looked at the horizon with binoculars then turned to Max.

"Are you sure the guy we're chasing is a killer?"

"He just killed two people, including the lighthouse keeper," said Max, matter-of-factly.

"This guy we're chasing killed the lighthouse keeper?"

"That's right."

The chief nodded. "Well, then we'll just have to catch him, won't we?"

They went back into the bridge and checked their position on the chart.

"He slipped away from the patrol boat. They've lost contact, but if that encounter slowed him up enough, we might be intercepting him any minute now."

"Yes," said Max, "if we figured it right."

"Of course," the chief continued, "finding him is one thing; keeping him from vanishing is another. You said you knew how to keep him from disappearing?"

"I think so," said Max. "I know he's using misdirection and assumptions, and I think I have an idea of how he's pulling it off. We'll just have to wait and see. Do you have a flare gun on board?"

"Sure. We keep a Very pistol right by the pilot house door."

"Good. Keep it handy," said Max.

"Misdirection and assumptions you said? Why do you say that?"

"Houdini told me."

As the rumrunner pounded its way northward, the two men were becoming more wary.

"The waves are picking up and slowing us down. If we get spotted again, we may not be able to outrun them."

"Then we'll just have to change course after we lose them. We'll get closer to the other shore and turn north from there. They'll still be looking over here."

"Bein' able to disappear sure comes in handy."

"Max, we should have seen them by now. I guess they're traveling faster than we thought. Either that or they went off in another direction."

Max paced the small area of the pilot house looking out into the night.

"No; if they were on course 340, that means they were heading northwards. Once they gave the other cutter the slip they would have returned to a similar course. I think we're going in the right direction, but they're a little faster than we'd hoped. We might still be gaining on them."

The chief nodded. "Well, a stern chase is a long chase. We'll keep on this course and hope we can catch up."

Yes, thought Max; here's hoping.

The men on the runner wedged themselves into the right corner behind the cabin to brace against the motion of the waves. They looked all around the horizon, but saw no sign of another boat. The engine droned on smoothly and everything was clear ahead. They relaxed a little.

"Looks like we gave them the slip."

"Yeah; another couple of hours and we'll be at the drop off point where we can get rid of the cargo."

"The coasties had me worried there for a minute, but they're miles away by now."

"Maybe we better cut the engine a minute and listen, just to be on the safe side."

"Good idea. Can't be too careful with a cargo like this."

They cut the engine and the boat slowed rapidly, wallowing drunkenly in the swells.

"I hear something to the south."

"Is it dying or getting louder?"

"Wait a minute... damn. It's getting louder. Whatever it is, it's heading this way. Let's get going!"

The engine sprang to life and the runner plowed onward, slamming into the waves. Soon, they heard another engine closing in on them.

"Brian, the Coast Guard. They're back! How did they find us?"

"It's a different cutter, maybe a six-bitter. We'll just have to fool them, too."

A few minutes later, a light from the cutter's searchlight cut through the darkness and started to illuminate the deck of the runner.

"All right. Get ready. It's time to disappear."

"I think that's our boy, Max," said the chief. "We're in firing range, but we'll fire over their heads. That should make them heave to fast enough."

"Yes. I can see them, but be on the alert for...Wow!"

A brilliant flash lit up the cutter. Everyone rubbed his eyes and refocused.

"They're gone!" shouted a lookout.

It was true. The searchlight stabbed ahead in the darkness and swung from side to side, but the sea was empty.

For a moment, even Max was disoriented, then he remembered misdirection and assumptions. That was the answer. It had to be.

"I guess you didn't have it figured out after all," said the chief. "He's done it again."

"Chief, grab the Very pistol and step out on deck. Hurry!"

"It won't do any good, Max. The searchlights can't find anything and they couldn't have gotten that far ahead."

"Never mind that, chief. Fire a flare over the stern."

"The stern?"

"Just do it...quickly!"

With a bang and a whoosh, the flare from the Very pistol rocketed into the blackness overhead. Max held his breath for a second, then the flare lit up the water behind the CG-182.

Max anxiously scanned the area and smiled.

There was the runner, heading in the opposite direction.

"I believe if you come about you can fire over their heads now chief," said Max. "They seem to have reappeared."

"Helmsman, come about. Gun crew prepare to fire over their heads."

The CG-182 swung about and crewmen started firing the foredeck gun.

"If she tries that disappearing runner trick again, we'll know what to do this time," said the chief.

"It doesn't look like it," said Max. "She's heaving to. You got her."

As the CG-182 pulled closer, Max saw two men standing on deck with their hands up. He ran to the rail.

"Hello, Brian," he said. "Come aboard."

John Reisinger

Chapter 23

The culprit

Coast Guardsmen swarmed over the runner. Brian and Patrick Murphy were handcuffed and placed under guard below decks on the CG-182, while a Coast Guardsman was left on the runner to take the rumrunner boat back to Crisfield.

Chief Voshel appeared along the rail.

"There you are, Max," said the chief. "How in the world did you know the runner would suddenly be behind us? We were looking ahead."

Max smiled. "That's what they were counting on. I've been thinking about the mysterious vanishing rumrunner and concluded it had to be done like a magic trick; by depending on misdirection and assumptions. The flash was their oversized searchlight shining in our eyes. Why would they do that? Misdirection. The light destroyed our night vision for a few seconds, temporarily blinding us. That way, they could make a radical course change and wind up behind us before our eyes became accustomed to the dark again. We made the assumption that they had to be in front of us because that's where they were when we last saw them, so we kept searching in front and wondering what happened to them."

"And the more we looked, the farther away they got," said the chief.

"Right. Then when they got far enough away, they just resumed their course as we pushed on ahead looking in the wrong direction. The only problem with the plan was that it caused them to lose a lot of time when they used it."

"Now, Max. You said this Brian Murphy killed the lighthouse keeper?"

"Yes, and Billy Thebold as well. That reminds me. Chief, could you get someone to get Brian Murphy's boots and bring them to the bridge? I want to have a look at them."

"His boots? If you say so, Max. I'll get someone to borrow them."

"By the way," said Max, "what was in that cargo that was so valuable the Murphy boys were willing to run it themselves? I had to be something more than the usual moonshine."

"This." He held up a bottle he had been holding. "We grabbed a couple of these for evidence. Take a look at the label. Canadian Club Finest Blended Canadian Whiskey. This isn't something some farmer cooked up with corn mash and some copper tubing; this is smooth, professionally blended, and aged in charred oak barrels. Stuff of this quality would be worth a fortune to one of the higher toned speakeasies. Apparently they were taking it to Annapolis for delivery to Washington. A cargo this valuable would be too tempting to trust to anyone else."

"And too profitable," Max added.

"The thing we can't figure out is where would someone on the Eastern Shore get quality Canadian whiskey?" said the chief. "Some of my crew think it's local rotgut with phony labels. Me, I'm not so sure the Murphys would risk their reputations by pawning off an inferior product. I think it's the real thing, but I have no idea how they got it here."

"I think I do," said Max. "But get me that boot first and then we can talk about it."

"Sure thing, Max."

The chief got back to the bridge in a few minutes. He had a pair of rubber boots in his hand.

"Here you are, Max; one pair of the best quality Lambertville rubber boots. What in the world do you want with these?"

Max didn't answer. He was examining the soles of the boots.

"Chief, do you have a magnifying glass handy?"

"Sure. Here you are. We keep one on the bridge for reading the fine points of charts."

Max looked some more, then smiled.

"Take a look at that."

The chief looked at the sole of the boot through the magnifying glass.

"It looks like a cut of some kind in the sole. Maybe he stepped on something," said the chief.

"How it got there isn't important. That cut helps to prove Brian Murphy killed Jack Coleman."

"But why would he want to kill Jack Coleman?" said the chief. "You already know Coleman wasn't tipping us off or informing on the runners."

"That's right; he wasn't informing the Coast Guard about the runners. That was an assumption again; an assumption a lot of people made."

"So then why did Murphy kill Jack Coleman?" said the chief.

"We were making another incorrect assumption. Coleman was using the radio sure enough, but he wasn't informing the Coast Guard about the runners, he was informing the runners about the Coast Guard."

"What?"

"I don't know all the details yet," said Max, "but it looks like Coleman was transmitting messages about Coast Guard patrols and coordinating deliveries with runners in the bay and with ships on Rum Row offshore. That's why he installed the longer range antenna. With the additional height of the lighthouse, he was able to get and send clear signals all that distance. I believe that Canadian whiskey is genuine, but they weren't able to smuggle a rum ship up in the bay so they ran it ashore on the Atlantic coast, trucked it to Crisfield, and the Murphy boys were going to run it the rest of the way for a fat profit. What's more, I think the whole thing was coordinated by the lighthouse keeper and his radio."

"Wait," said the chief. "If Coleman was doing all that for the Murphys and was that valuable, why kill him?"

"I think I know that, too, but why don't we have a word with the Murphys. Maybe they'll be in a talkative mood. Chief, you have law enforcement powers don't you?"

The chief shrugged. "That's what President Coolidge says."

"Good. You can question the Murphys and I'll assist."

The Murphys were handcuffed and guarded in the crew area below, a smallish section with a communal table in the middle and bunks along the sides.

The Murphys looked up at Max and the chief sullenly.

"Now, boys," said the chief in an official tone, "we'd like to have a little chat with you before we get back."

Max mumbled something to the chief.

"Did you injure your arm, Mr. Murphy? I see a bandage."

Brian Murphy hastily rolled down his sleeve over the bandage."

"I cut myself a couple of weeks ago. It's nothing."

The chief stepped aside and gave Max his turn.

"I'm afraid it's time to come clean about Jack Coleman," said Max.

"I don't know what you're talking about," said Brian.

"I'm talking about a knife that was left at the light house, a knife you purchased from Pat Dolan in Cambridge last year. I'm talking about the bandage on your arm and the knife wound that it no doubt covers, a wound that was the source of the blood found at the lighthouse."

Brian Murphy remained silent. Patrick Murphy looked terrified.

"And," Max continued in a softer voice, "I'm talking about your boots."

Murphy looked up sharply. "Yeah; what about my boots? Some swab jockey came and took them."

"I'm sorry, Brian, but they'll have to be held as evidence now."

"Evidence? What do you mean?"

"You should have been more careful at the lighthouse, Brian; maybe cleaned up a little more. It seems you stepped in some of that small puddle of blood you left by the body and left a perfect boot print. Sergeant Bentley has a close up photo of it. The photo shows that the tread has a small diagonal cut in it, a cut that matches one on your boots exactly. So unless you're going to claim that someone else used your knife and wore your boots and then cut your arm, I'm afraid the police have all the evidence they need to hang you."

Patrick, who had been listening with rising panic, suddenly blurted out. "It wasn't Brian's fault. Jack Coleman was trying to blackmail us!"

"Shut up, Patrick!" Brian snapped.

"Yes," said Max. "That's what Billy Thebold told me that day near the pool hall, and that's why he had to be killed, wasn't it? You overheard Billy and decided he couldn't be trusted to keep your secret, so you took him for a one way boat ride, probably in the same boat you used tonight."

Patrick hunched over and put his face in his hands. Brian remained silent.

"If you tell us about it, it might help you when your trial comes up, Brian. We have the boots, the knife, and the motive. I have no doubt they can find a fingerprint or two at the lighthouse if they try. I know what you did and why, but I'd be interested in your side."

Brian was silent a few more seconds, then he seemed to come to a decision.

"All right. I got nothing to lose at this point anyway. Jack Coleman was using his souped up radio to keep us in touch with Rum Row and to let us know when the Coast Guard was in the area. Then we started arranging for special shipments from the offshore fleet to Tom's Cove on Chincoteague. From there it was short haul to Crisfield. Then someone would run it across the bay to D.C. or Annapolis or Baltimore."

"So what happened to this cozy arrangement?"

"Jack Coleman happened. He got greedy. Suddenly he wanted to triple his cut. We couldn't pay him that much; we got expenses to cover and bribes to pay, but he insisted. We had Billy Thebold working a radio to try to do the same thing and make the final arrangements, but Jack said he'd tell all to the Prohibition police and to the Coast Guard if we didn't pay up. He'd claim we had forced him to do the radio work! Can you beat that?"

"No honor among thieves. So how did it end up in murder?"

"I keep smellin' coffee. Somebody get me a cup and I'll tell you."

The chief motioned to the guard, who came back with a steaming white mug. Brian drank deeply.

"Ahhh. That's the stuff. Nothin' like some good java. Well, anyway, I went to see Jack. I went at night so nobody would see me and make the connection. When he opened the door he had a knife in his hand, I almost fell off the walkway. Turns out he was on his guard in case Tom Paisley showed up as he'd threatened. When he saw it was me, he relaxed and let me in. We sat and had coffee and chatted, real civil-like. I tried to explain how unreasonable his demands were, but he just got mad about it; said he deserved it because he was takin' all the risks. I don't know how he figured that, seein' as how other people were runnin' the stuff, but that's what he thought. He said the Coast Guard was getting better at findin' radios and he was in increasing danger, so he had to make his money while he could. I tried to reason with him, but he got himself convinced. I guess sitting in that lighthouse, he had a lot of time on his hands. Anyway, he starts poundin' on the table and I get up to leave, then he grabs me by the shirt and starts shakin' me and pushin' me."

"What did you do then?"

"I pushed back. Next thing I know, we're havin' a knock down drag out fight, punching and throwing things. I pulled out my knife to try to calm him down and he grabbed that kitchen knife and went after me. Well, I backed away and tripped over something we'd knocked on the floor. He slashed at me with that knife and cut my arm. I was bleedin' by now; not real bad, but steady. I fell backward and must have dropped my knife. So I grabbed a piece of firewood from a bin there and swung at him. I hit him several times before he went down, but he finally did. By the time I caught my breath, I could see he was dead, so I went through the place and removed anything that could tie him to me, including his log book and most important, his code book he used for his radio work. I guess I left blood drips all over the place and even stepped in some. I got some towels from the bath room and wrapped my arm and got out of there. I didn't even realize I didn't have my knife until I was back in Crisfield. I figured anyone who found it would think it was his."

Max looked at the chief, who was wide eyed at this tale.

What about Billy?" Max asked.

"I hated to do it, but Billy kept flappin' his jaw. He even told people he was a radio operator. I warned him lots of times and with Jack Coleman dead, I was even more nervous about loose talk. Then when I heard him tell you about Coleman's blackmail scheme, I knew I had to do something before Billy blabbed the rest. So I took him out on a boat and coshed him near the light, so maybe people would think it was Virginia drudgers."

He looked upward and turned his head.

"We're changing course. We must be near the Devil's Elbow light."

In the darkness, the lighthouse was a silhouette with a white beam slowly turning from its roof. Ripples from the wake of the CG-182 drifted in serene parallel ridges and splashed gently on the piles. In the blackness overhead, the stars had come out, cold points of light scattered in a moonless night sky as the Devil's Elbow light receded in the distance behind the boat.

John Reisinger

Chapter 24

Settling scores

It was well after midnight when the CG-182 gently bumped up against the steamboat pier in Crisfield.

"Well, rumrunning's a crime, but murder's a bit more serious," said the chief, "so I think we should turn the Murphys over to Sergeant Bentley. He can work out the jurisdiction with the federal boys."

The chief sent a crewman to Fred Bentley's house a few blocks away and presently, the sergeant appeared, tired and dirty.

"Dang it Max; do you mean to tell me you nabbed the real killer while me and my deputies were sloggin' and swattin' mosquitos over on Bloodsworth?"

Max smiled. "I'm afraid so, Fred. Oh, and here are Brian Murphy's boots. Hang onto them tight, they're evidence."

Sergeant Bentley took the boots. "Brian Murphy? Well, don't that just beat all? Where are you keepin' him?"

"He's enjoying the hospitality of the U.S. Coast Guard at the moment, courtesy of Chief Voshel and his able crew. He's agreed to turn them both over to you. Do you have any room in the jail?"

"Absolutely. Soons I let Nell Paisley out. Bring 'em on over and we'll get 'em fixed up. How in the devil did you..."

"I'll tell you all about it, Fred, but there's something I have to do first."

He turned to Chief Voshel

"Thanks again, chief. If it weren't for you and your boys, those two would be still at large. I'm in your debt. If there's ever anything I can do..."

The chief grinned. "Forget it, Max. That's what we get paid for. Besides, catching the disappearing runner will provide us with sea stories for years to come."

They stepped off the CG-182 and walked to Sergeant Bentley's office.

Inside, Allison was curled up on the cot of the empty jail cell wrapped in a coarse gray blanket with Crisfield PD stenciled on it. Beside her was a small pile of papers. Max picked them up and read.

*Conclusion of spiritualism article,
by Allison Hurlock*

People have clung to the idea of communicating with the dead since the dawn of time. Scientists, the newspapers, and even experts such as Houdini have exposed spiritualists time after time, but somehow, it seems to make no difference. No amount of contrary evidence, exposés, phony spiritualists, or swindlers can quite crush out the idea. When one spiritualist is exposed as a fake, people simply go to another. But why?

> *When we encounter something that is this long lasting and this resistant to undermining and debunking, maybe something else is going on; something where the return on emotional investment outweighs mere rationality. Maybe in some cases at least, spiritualism, for all its phoniness, gives back something unexplained and wonderful. Maybe spiritualism can sometimes do what nothing else can for those who have a void in their hearts because of the loss of a loved one. Maybe spiritualism can provide that most elusive but essential of commodities: peace of mind.*
> *So is spiritualism phony, or is it real?*
> *Everything we know of spiritualism tells us that as a means of communicating with the dead, spiritualism is pretty much phony, but as a means of therapy and healing, spiritualism is very real indeed*

"So how do you like it?" came a sleepy voice. Allison was awake and looking at him. Strands of her auburn hair hung over her face.

"It's great. Your stuff keeps getting better and better."

"Flattery will get you everywhere. Did you catch Brian Murphy?"

"Yes, and he's waiting to use this cell. Sorry."

"Oh. Well, let me get out, then. I'd rather not have a homicidal room mate."

Sergeant Bertley and the chief from the CG-182 escorted the Murphys to the cell Allison had been using and locked the door with a loud clang.

"Let's take a walk," said Max. "Sergeant Bentley and the chief have some paperwork to do and we'd just be in the way."

They walked down by the dock and watched the crew securing the CG-182.

"So the case is solved?"

"Pretty much," said Max. "Now J.D. and Casper won't have to turn their life savings over to Gaston Means."

"Oh, Max. I didn't have a chance to tell you. They brought me here, and they came to pay Gaston Means. They were on their way over to his place this afternoon. I'm sorry."

"Oh, no," said Max. "J.D. and Casper paid that rat? I let them down, Allison. I solved the case a few hours too late. It'll be a pretty poor sort of justice if the killers are locked up and the boys lose their homes and life savings. And all because I didn't come through in time."

Max stood moodily with his hands in his pockets and his head hanging. Allison placed her hand on his arm.

"You did everything you could, Max. Nobody could have done better. You were miles ahead of the police. Things just didn't work out. It's not a perfect world. That's what you always tell me, isn't it? You try to live a good life; you try to do what's right, but sometimes no matter what you do, the bad guys win anyway."

"I know, but that doesn't make it any easier."

They were near the steamboat pier and looking at the workboats tied up for the night. Suddenly, Max stopped.

"That looks like the Karen Rebecca."

He walked over to the battered white workboat and saw that it was indeed the Karen Rebecca. But where were J.D. and Casper?

"J.D....Casper. Are you in there?"

"Max, is that you?" came a sleepy voice.

J.D. and Casper appeared, yawning and stretching from the shadows where they had been sleeping.

"Hey, Max. We figured it was too late to head back, so we thought we'd wait until morning..."

"Never mind that," Max interrupted. "Allison says you came here to give the money to Gaston Means."

"Well, yes, Max. We saw him this afternoon. I mean, this was the deadline, so we figured..."

"Oh, no. Fellas, I'm sorry I let you down. I just..."

"How's that, Max?" said Casper, who seemed to be slightly more awake than J.D.

"I didn't solve the case in time and now Means has your life savings. Now you have to start over and..."

"Means ain't got a thing, Max," said J.D.

"What? But you said you went over there to give him the money. Wasn't he there?"

"Oh, he was there, all right, and fair droolin' over the cash, but it was the damndest thing...oh, excuse me Miz Allison...anyway, the thing is, he wouldn't take it."

"Wouldn't take it?"

"He said he figured that Smith guy was a fraud and he didn't want us to be inconvenienced; said it wouldn't look good in the papers. Ain't that the limit, though?"

Max smiled. "Worried about how it would look in the newspapers, huh? Now where did he get that idea?"

Casper put his hand on Max's shoulder.

"Actually, Max, he said you convinced him. Thanks."

"Whew!" said Allison. "Talk about your happy endings..."

Sergeant Bentley released Nell Paisley, locked up the Murphys, then met Max and Allison at the dock.

"I don't know how you did it, Max, but those boys are singin' like canaries. I knew they were up to their necks in bootleggin' but seems like they got themselves an empire almost."

"Not for long. What about Tom Paisley?" said Max.

"Shoot. We spent hours muckin' through the wetlands on Bloodsworth. The only thing that's could hide there would be a mosquito."

Max nodded. "I thought so. Brian Murphy's so called tip was just a ploy to send you and your deputies north while he ran liquor to the south."

"Misdirection again?"

"Exactly."

"That stuff really works. So where in the devil is Tom Paisley?"

"I imagine he's within a mile or so of his brother's house," said Max. "But I wouldn't worry about it. I'm sure now that Nell has been released, she'll find a way to get the word to him that the coast is clear. He'll be back before you know it."

"Yeah, and fightin' all over again, no doubt. He'll chase other women and she'll chase other men and occasionally I'll get dragged into it to settle things down. Well, at least they didn't kill anybody."

"It all comes with the territory, Fred."

"Say, it's almost one AM. It's too late to find a hotel. Why don't you and Allison come over to my place and bed down in the spare room for the night? The missus would be glad to have you."

"I thought you'd never ask," said Max.

They slept until past nine, then enjoyed a hearty breakfast courtesy of Fred Bentley's wife. Then Fred Bentley drove them out to their airplane for the trip home.

"Thanks again, Max. I'd have clapped Tom Paisley in jail if it wasn't for you."

"Don't thank me yet," said Max. You still have to deal with the Bureau of Investigation, the Coast Guard, and the Lighthouse Service over who has jurisdiction for what. I did the easy part."

"Well, at least I know I have the right man in jail. Goodbye, Max. Goodbye Allison."

They climbed into the cockpit and started the engine.

"Max," said Allison over the sound of the engine. "I don't remember Gypsy ever sounding this smooth. What happened?"

"Rufus Grace is what happened. I gave him ten dollars to give Gypsy a going over while I was in Crisfield. The man is a genius with motors. I have a feeling that once his reputation starts to spread, he'll never have to run bootleg again."

She shook her head. "Max, you do move in mysterious ways."

A minute later they were in the sky heading toward St Michaels. Below them, another train pulled out of Crisfield carrying another cargo of oysters.

John Reisinger

Chapter 25

Harold Johnson's last gift

When they arrived home, Max found the note Allison left him in Sergeant Bentley's office and the note Allison received from Thelma Dalrymple.

"Say, why don't we put these notes in our trophy room upstairs?" he asked Allison.

"A top drawer idea, Max. I can put them on some matting and frame them. We can hang them right above the bootlegger address book from the Moorestown case and next to our certificate of membership in the Jekyll Island Club."

"Yes sir, it's getting to be a regular black museum, or maybe a chamber of horrors. Soon, we'll be able to charge admission."

"So when will you be available to pose for your marble statue?"

Three months later, after Brian Murphy was tried and convicted, Max and Allison held a get together at home to celebrate the conclusion of the case and to tie up some loose ends. It was a cold day, and the house was crowded, but a fire burned cheerfully in the fireplace as the wind blew outside. Among the guests were Isis Dalrymple, Duffy Merkle, Mabel Johnson, Thelma Lonnigan, and of course, J.D. Pratt and Casper Nowitsky.

"All hail the Eastern Shore's premier detecting duo," announced Isis, raising a glass of punch. "When they are around, no criminal is safe and no secret goes un examined. Move over Sherlock Holmes; move over Lord Peter Whimsey; move over Philo Vance. The Hurlocks have you beat!"

"Hear, hear!" said the others.

Max turned to Allison.

"See. Now this is exactly the sort of thing I was talking about. More crazy celebrity talk and hero worship. It's getting out of hand. We may have to move."

"Oh, let them have their fun. Lord knows there are few enough celebrities in St Michaels. Everyone around here is either a waterman, a tomato farmer, or a chicken farmer. All honorable and vital professions, of course, but the closest we get to celebrity is when the Adams Floating Theater is tied up in town."

Max was not appeased. "I'm not arguing how wonderful it is to have celebrities rattling around, I just don't want to be one of them."

Duffy Merkle appeared next to them.

"Max, that was a good job of detective work, but with the Murphy's gone, I gotta find my own runners now."

"I'm afraid I can't help you there, Duffy," Max said. "Still, there should be plenty of others out there. I imagine you'll have them lined up at your door before too long."

"Oh, I already do," said Duffy. My problem is picking out which ones I want to use."

"How about Rufus Grace?"

"Rufus? Shoot; Rufus has so much work fixin' up boat engines nowadays, he ain't got time for runnin'."

Thelma Lonnigan had Casper Nowitsky cornered by the front stairs and was giving him the inside story on the state of local telecommunications. "I tell you, Casper, with more and more folks getting telephones around here, they'll have to hire more operators pretty soon. Lands sakes; the switchboard is starting to look like a bowl of spaghetti some days. It's more than one woman can handle."

"Oh, Max," said Allison. "We got a letter today. Here I think you'll be interested."

Max looked at the letter.

> *Dear Max and Allison:*
> *I read in the paper that you figured out the disappearing boat trick. Too bad; I could have used it in my act. Congratulations anyway.*
> *Houdini*
> *P.S. I understand it involved a searchlight and a sudden course change. Interesting, but that's not how I would have done it.*

Max nodded with satisfaction. "Well, at least the quality of our correspondence is improving. Even our letters involve celebrity, it seems."

J.D. was telling the others about the hair-raising events that lead to the solving of the twin murders. What his account lacked in accuracy it made up for in sensation.

"...and they ran down the killers on the high seas, just like in the movies. Miz Allison went under cover and found the boat! She's a hero, too."

"Wait a minute," said Allison. "That's not exactly…"

"Now you know how it feels," said Max.

Casper tapped Max on the shoulder. "I read in the papers that the Bureau of Investigation got itself a new director a couple of months ago, a fella name of J. Edgar Hoover," he said with obvious satisfaction. "First thing he did was fire Gaston Means."

Max nodded. "I've been following that. They pulled him in on a congressional hearing and Means lied as usual. He's been tried and found guilty of perjury. He got two years in jail."

Casper and J.D. shook their heads. "That's a good place for him. You were sure right about not givin' him any money, Max."

When things had settled down, Allison and Isis Dalryple brought out the fried chicken and everyone sat down at several makeshift tables. Although Allison's cooking skills were somewhat limited, Isis was an authority on the proper preparation of southern fried chicken, and the smell coming from the small kitchen had everyone salivating at the expected meal.

When the golden pieces were finally served, everyone took them eagerly.

"This is great. Too bad we can't have beer to go with it," said J.D.

"Beer?" said Duffy Merkle. "That can be arranged. How many gallons you want?"

"By the way" said Max. "I read a Coast Guard report that said you guys were picked up out on the bay at night and you claimed you were fishing. What gives?"

"Well, gee, Max," said Casper, reaching for a drumstick. "A fella has to make a livin', don't he?"

"Never mind," Max sighed.

Death at the Lighthouse

Later, when the chicken had been reduced to plates with piles of bones, Max stood up and thanked everyone for coming and for their help in bringing the case to a successful close.

"You're all our friends and we appreciate your help. We couldn't have done it without you."

When the applause died down, Mabel Johnson stood up and asked to speak. Max and Allison looked at each other curiously, then agreed.

"As you all know, I've had a rough time of it since my husband Harold died. I can barely get by with workin' at the cannery, but it's all I got and I have to live with it. Well Harold, God rest his soul, left me a shuckin' knife that I use every day. Miz Allison and Mr. Max noticed the knife and used it to track down a knife belonging to the killer. It wasn't much and I was glad to help out. Well, this morning I got this letter from The United States Lighthouse Service. Mr. Max, would you read it to everybody?

Max took the letter.

> *Dear Mrs. Johnson:*
> *As you are no doubt aware, the United States Lighthouse Service offered a reward for anyone with information leading to the identity and punishment of whomever was responsible for the death of Jack Coleman, keeper of the Devil's Elbow light.*
>
> *The guilty party has now been brought to justice through the efforts of Maxwell Hurlock of St Michaels, Maryland. Mr. Hurlock has assured us that it was information you provided that led him to this conclusion, so we are acting on his recommendation and awarding you the $ 5,000. Congratulations and thank you.*
>
> *The U.S. Lighthouse Service*

Max looked up and saw Mabel Johnson crying, along with nearly everyone else.

"I want everyone to know what Mr. Max and Miz Allison did for me," she said between sobs. "My husband gave me a gift when he left me that knife, but Mr. Max and Miz Allison were the ones who made Harold's gift into gold."

Isis Dalrymple then led the crowd in a rousing chorus of "For they are jolly good fellows."

Allison leaned over to Max.

"Well, Max, what do you think? Maybe being a local celebrity isn't so bad after all."

He slipped his arm around her and raised his glass in salute to their friends.

"Maybe not," said Max. "Maybe not."

The End

Notes

The Lighthouse Murder

Death at the Lighthouse is fiction, but is based on a real case; the death of lighthouse keeper Ulman Owens at the Holland Island Bar light in 1931. The Holland Island Bar light was on the approach to Crisfield, Maryland, and was a screw pile light. On March 11, 1931 someone noticed the light was out and notified a passing ship, whose first mate, along with the captain of a Crisfield oyster boat went to the light to investigate. They found Ulman Owens dead and a scene of devastation that looked as if a fight had taken place. There was blood splattered around and a bloody butcher knife on the floor, but no wounds on Owens.

Rumors soon spread of vengeful rumrunners, jealous husbands, and jailhouse confessions, but an autopsy determined Owens had an enlarged heart and the death was attributed to natural causes. The autopsy also determined Owens had a cracked skull, but this was decided to be a result of some sort of dying seizure. The blood was never explained and the case was closed.

The Holland Island Bar light was damaged by a mistaken rocket attack by Navy Skyraiders the night of February 19, 1957. The pilots had mistaken the light for a nearby hulk that was used for target practice. The lighthouse was replaced by an automated beacon in 1960.

Oystering on the Chesapeake Bay (Chapter 1)

Although oysters had been a popular product of the Chesapeake Bay since before Europeans came, the invention of a process for canning oysters in the late 1800s, coupled with steam powered shipping and the discovery of massive oyster beds in Tangier Sound led to a boom in the industry. Crisfield, Maryland became a boom town, especially after a railroad connection was established in 1868. Crisfield, Oxford, Cambridge, and St Michaels sprouted packing houses along their waterfronts to get in on the demand. Baltimore had even more packing houses. The oyster boom led to the "Oyster Wars" between oystermen of Maryland and Virginia when Virginia Oystermen came north to dredge Maryland oyster beds, causing both depletion and environmental damage. Maryland even established an "Oyster Navy" to patrol and control the mayhem. To limit the damage, Maryland law only allowed oyster dredging by boats under sail, leading to the development and use of the graceful Skipjacks that can still be seen today.

By the 1920s, the oyster wars had calmed down, and the frantic overharvesting had caused oyster production to drop, but watermen all over Maryland's Eastern Shore still made their living by harvesting oysters in the winter and blue crabs in the summer.

Rumrunning on the Chesapeake (Chapter 3)

With its miles of inlets, creeks and rivers and its proximity to Baltimore, Annapolis, Washington D.C. and Virginia, Maryland's Eastern Shore was a natural haven for blockade runners and smugglers ever since the Civil War. During Prohibition, Maryland's long tradition of moonshining was added to the mix and the result was a hotbed of bootlegging and rumrunning up and down the Chesapeake Bay from Virginia to Baltimore.

The local watermen had boats and extensive knowledge of the waterways, so many became rumrunners, at least occasionally. The Coast Guard was spread thinly and lots of freshly made liquor made its way to speakeasies in Baltimore, Annapolis, Washington, D.C. and beyond. In addition, ships full of foreign imported liquor loitered beyond the three mile limit waiting to smuggle their goods ashore. Some ships of the rum fleet snuck into the Chesapeake to waiting runners and unloaded their cargo there, but most of the running was to and from the Eastern Shore.

Spiritualism (Chapter 4)

A belief in the possibility of communicating with the spirits of the dead has been around for many years, but really started in 1849 when the Fox sisters in upstate New York claimed to have contacted the spirit of a dead peddler and produced loud knocking noises to prove it. Though the sisters later admitted it was a hoax, the movement was off and running. Spiritualism was so well established that Mary Todd Lincoln had several séances conducted in the White House. Spiritualism faded somewhat by the turn of the century, but got a revival during the First World War when so many grieving relatives yearned to communicate with sons, husbands, and fathers who had been killed.

Mediums conducted séances at their residences, in private homes, and even in theaters and summer camps. Despite the fact that a few notable people such as Arthur Conan Doyle became believers, spiritualism attracted many skeptics and debunkers such as

Houdini. Even so, for some bereaved people, spiritualism provided comfort and hope, even if it sometimes did so at a steep price.

One of the biggest centers for spiritualism was and still is, Lily Dale, New York. The home of a large spiritualist summer camp on Cassadaga Lake, Lily Dale became a spiritualist center when spiritualists moved the childhood home of the Fox sisters there in 1927. Lily Dale still bills itself as the "World's largest center for the religion of spiritualism." and is the home of the National Association of Spiritualist Churcles, a nationwide association of spiritualists.

Crisfield and the oyster boom (Chapter 9)

With the discovery of vast oyster beds in adjacent Tangier Sound coupled with new canning methods, steamship transportation and the construction of a railroad line, Crisfield became an oyster boom town in the late 1800s, shipping canned oysters all over the country and the world. Other towns on the Chesapeake Bay got into the act as well, with canneries springing up in Baltimore, Annapolis, St Michaels, and Cambridge, but Crisfield was the biggest.

With so much unregulated wealth up for grabs, rampant crime and corruption gave Crisfield the nickname of the "Dodge City of the East". In 1910, more boats were registered in Crisfield than in any other port in the United States, and one packing company employed 2,000 oyster shuckers. Out on the bay, watermen fought over prime oyster beds, sometimes with guns. Maryland set up the Oyster Police to try to control the chaos.

Death at the Lighthouse

By the 1920s, when this story takes place, the oyster boom had slackened due to over harvesting without regard to replenishment, but in spite of declining harvests, Crisfield was still shipping lots of oysters, as much as 60,000 gallons in a single day. Today, Crisfield still ships oysters, but is better known for crabs.

Gaston Means (Chapter 9)

Gaston Means was a confidence man greatly skilled at telling false stories with great conviction. He started off as a private detective who constantly uncovered fantastic "clues" that needed further expensive investigation. At one point, he swindled a wealthy widow out of a considerable sum. When the widow suddenly died at a firing range Means had taken her to, the coroner said it was no accident and Means was tried for murder. He was acquitted by a sympathetic home town jury and then went to trial for forging the woman's will. He gained immunity by promising, but not delivering, a trunk full of German spy documents. He became a private detective for William Burns and the Burns detective agency, then a federal investigator when Burns was appointed head of the Bureau of Investigation. (Federal was not added to the agency's title until years later.)

During Prohibition, Means took fees from bootleggers to issue liquor permits and to fix their legal problems with the government. In 1924, however, Means was fired from the Bureau of Investigation by its new head, J. Edgar Hoover. That same year, congress investigated lax Prohibition enforcement and Means went to jail for perjury. In jail, he wrote a tell-all book accusing President Harding's widow of murdering him, a book he repudiated once the royalties dried up.

Means next project was a group of New Yorkers concerned about Russian espionage. Means convinced them he knew of a spy ring and a secret cache of documents contained in 24 trunks (trunks seemed to be popular with Means) and 11 suitcases, and offered to investigate for $100 a day. After a three year investigation, Means announced that the Soviet agents had burned the documents.

After the Lindbergh baby was kidnapped in 1932, Means assured Evalyn Walsh McLean, wife of Washington Post heir Edward McLean and owner of the Hope diamond, that he could get the baby returned. After taking over $100,000 from her with no baby to show for it, Means was found guilty of grand larceny and was sent to Leavenworth, where he died in 1938.

J. Millard Tawes (Chapter 9)

After working in various businesses owned by his family, J. Millard Tawes was elected Clerk of the Court for Somerset County, Maryland in 1930. He went on to be elected State Comptroller, then Governor of Maryland from 1959 to 1967. Among his initiatives as governor were programs to help sustain oyster production in the Chesapeake Bay.

Houdini (Chapter 17)

The Great Houdini was born Erik Weisz in Hungary, but grew up in Appleton, Wisconsin. After renaming himself after French magician Robert

Houdin, Houdini started as a card act with occasional handcuff escapes. Later, when he concentrated on escapes, his career took off. His escapes included escaping from a milk can, escaping from a jail cell, escaping from a sealed canvas mail sack, and escaping from a chained wooden crate dumped off of a pier. In addition to his skill in magic, Houdini had a genius for showmanship and for milking the last drop of excitement out of a situation. His trick of passing through a masonry wall is less well known today, but was a sensation at the time. His magic tricks were sensational enough, but he combined them with an unerring sense of showmanship that has seldom been equaled. He knew how to gage an audience and how to squeeze the greatest level of excitement and suspense from his act. His tricks were usually met with thunderous applause and cheers.

Houdini dabbled in spiritualism and arranged code words with his wife and friends to authenticate any communications after death. He was very close to his mother and started going to séances as a way of communicating with her after she died, but easily saw through the fakes and soon began a crusade to expose them. Houdini died of appendicitis on Halloween night, 1926, just two years after this story takes place. His wife Beth held séances every Halloween night for ten years after his death attempting to communicate with him. The last séance, on the tenth anniversary of his death, was held on the roof of the Knickerbocker Hotel in Hollywood, and was also unsuccessful, although it ended with a huge thunderstorm that supposedly occurred nowhere else in the area.

H.L. Mencken (Chapter 18)

The "Sage of Baltimore" was one of the most influential writers of the twentieth century. He is best known for writing The American Language, a multi-volume study, and a series of biting satirical dispatches from the Scopes "Monkey" Trial. He was the inspiration for the character of E.K. Hornbeck in the play Inherit the Wind.

Mencken was not sympathetic to democracy, but he was to the German cause in the First World War. He was famous for scathing condemnation of what he considered ignorant middle classes, which he called the "Booboise", especially in the American south. He once referred to Arkansas as the "apex of moronia."

Mencken was full of opinionated contradictions. He believed in Anglo-Saxon superiority, yet wrote a blistering editorial condemning people for not stopping a lynching. He supported Germany and Germans in many areas, but called Hitler a buffoon. Unlike many intellectuals during the 1930s, he had no affection for the Soviets and wrote that compared to Stalin, "Hitler was hardly more than a common Ku Kluxer and Mussolini almost a philanthropist." His writings display touches of anti-Semitism, but he condemned persecution of the Jews in Germany, and criticized Roosevelt for not accepting Jewish refugees.

He died in 1956, bequeathing his books and papers to Baltimore's Enoch Pratt Free Library.

Arthur and Franklin Perdue (Chapter 19)

Arthur Perdue's egg business grew to become Perdue Farms, one of the most successful chicken businesses on the Eastern Shore, and the third largest producer of broiler chickens in the U.S. Arthur Perdue's reluctance to accrue debt kept him from expanding as fast as he could have, but even so, he and wife Pearl built a hatchery in 1925 and the business grew from there. Later, son Frank, whose advertising motto was "It takes a tough man to make a tender chicken" took the business to the position it enjoys today and supported the Franklin Perdue School of Business College at Salisbury University that was established in 1986.

About the author

John Reisinger is a former Coast Guard officer and engineer. He lives with his wife and research partner Barbara on Maryland's Eastern Shore. John writes and speaks on a wide range of historical, crime, writing and technical topics, and is the author of several books, including Master Detective, Death of a Flapper, Death on a Golden Isle, Nassau, and Evasive Action.

And don't miss other adventures of Max and Allison Hurlock as they investigate murder and mayhem among the well-to-do in the Roaring 20s.

Death of a Flapper- How did the most popular girl in town and her ex-fiancée wind up dead in her locked bedroom?

Death on a Golden Isle- Murder crashes the party at an exclusive island club for millionaires off the Georgia coast.

And coming soon...

Death and the Blind Tiger- Ellsworth Connelly had it all, a grand house in New York, racehorses, and the money to pursue every woman he met. Along the way he left a vengeful ex-wife and trail of jilted women, jealous husbands, and resentful business partners. Is it any wonder he wound up dead in his own parlor? Now Max and Allison must travel to New York City, with its speakeasies, literary lights, gangsters and corruption. Max becomes the target of bootleggers while locking horns with the New York Police and Allison goes to lunch at the Algonquin round table to solve a case with too many suspects. Their only clue is a blindfolded ceramic tiger...sent by the dead man!

Based on a real case, Death and the Blind Tiger is a roar through the Roaring 20s.

Other books by John Reisinger....
See www.johnreisinger.com for more detail

Master Detective:

The Life and Crimes of Ellis Parker,
America's Real-life Sherlock Holmes

The story of America's greatest detective and his tragic role in the Lindbergh kidnapping investigation. He obtained a signed confession but went to prison for his trouble.

"...thoroughly researched, well-crafted biography ...Gripping." Booklist

"Fascinating reading for true crime fans and mystery buffs alike."....Max Allan Collins, author of The Road to Perdition.

"...a masterpiece of a biography." ... Troy Soos, author of The Gilded Cage.

"...a story powerfully told."...Roger Johnson, in the newsletter of the Sherlock Holmes Society of London.

"Very well done…an important and entertaining book. ..great accomplishment." Jim Fisher, author of The Lindbergh Case

Evasive Action:

The Hunt for Gregor Meinhoff

A tense manhunt through WWII Canada for an escaped German POW with an explosive secret that could change the outcome of the war.

"Fast paced, well-constructed..a first-rate adventure yarn." … John Goodspeed, Easton Star-Democrat book review.

Nassau

Civil War blockade runners turn a sleepy tropical port into a boomtown as they await their next runs through the fire and steel of the deadly Union blockade.

"the final chase scene was among the most exciting things I've ever read." … Dr. Ken Startup, history professor and VP for Academic Affairs, Williams Baptist College.

Reading group guide for

Death at the Lighthouse

As the story progressed, what character did you suspect was the killer and why?

When Max discovered the new aerial at the lighthouse, did you think it figured into the crime? How?

Discuss the underground economy that developed on the Eastern Shore as a result of Prohibition.

What sort of red herrings appear in the story and which are most convincing?

How does the unique character of Crisfield affect the story?

John Reisinger

How would the investigation of the murder have been handled differently with today's technology?

In what ways are Max and Allison a reflection of the 1920s and of their backgrounds?

Do you agree with Madame DeSousa's justification for her deceptions to her clients? Why or why not?

How do you think Houdini got to the other side of the brick wall in his show?

How do Allison and Max work as a team and how do they sometimes come in conflict?